ONE FLIGHT ✈ FICTION ™

BREAKING STRIDE

STEPHEN PASKE

Edited by Christy Parr

Printed in the United States of America
First Printing: September 2006

Library of Congress Control Number: 2006930911

ISBN-13: 978-0-9773175-5-4
ISBN-10: 0-9773175-5-2

To Coach Deane
Still a Source of Inspiration

Chapter I

Seventy meters short of the most stunning upset in the history of the State Mile, the Cuban's lead looked indestructible. What nobody knew was that he'd be dead before he crossed the finish line.

It started with a miniscule black spot firing across his retina. Five steps later, a shower of blurs flooded his eyes. He was stone sober, but couldn't have passed a sobriety test. The crowd gaped in horror, as he helplessly wobbled out to lane four.

The Cuban collapsed 40 meters short of the finish. Thirty meters behind, Rod hesitated. His stride relaxed. Demoralized by the boy's mid-race surge, he'd settled into second place. Now, fate thrust him into the role of leader. Not for long. An opportunistic sophomore from Wayzata materialized on his outside shoulder and burst into a ferocious kick.

Stunned, Rod fell back two strides. He had already accepted his fate, another red ribbon in the State Mile. But not in this fashion. Not to some sophomore, who had only reached this position by gutlessly laying back at the start. The Cuban had earned the right to the blue ribbon.

His 59-second third lap was the definition of courage. But now that he'd faltered, who was this?

Rod narrowed his eyes on the back of the sophomore's blue singlet. He craved inspiration. He needed an opening. Sixty meters remained, but it seemed he just lacked the will to cut into the gap. Then he saw it. Improperly fitted, the sophomore's singlet slipped off his right shoulder. Up went his arm to adjust it. Rod pounced.

Such a grimace. The veins of his neck looked like they would burst through the skin. Head tilted upwards, Rod gnashed his teeth with such force that he chipped the enamel. It felt like fine sand on his taste buds, a welcome change from the faint flavor of blood seeping up from the back of his throat.

Acid plumed through his legs. Rod fought. One grating step at a time, he drove his knees forward, pumping his arms with authority. If the legs lost their will, then the arms would just have to pull all the harder. This was a lesson not yet learned by his closest competitor. Fixing a uniform meant a break in good form. Rod punished him.

Neck and neck, the two runners rumbled toward home. The Cuban lay helplessly sprawled in lane three. Selfishly, ruthlessly, they passed the limp body without hesitation. Thirty-five meters remained. Their separation could be measured in thousandths of seconds. Their eyes met. Rod saw victory.

He also saw anguish, fear, pain, and suffering. He suffered. But not like the sophomore. Experience taught him to block it, ignore it, stomp it out like a fire. He could see the sophomore lacked such experience. He was caught in the present, trapped in his body, unable to become just a mind.

Pain is immediate, instant, and unbearable. It originates in the nerves of the body, while those same nerves order it stopped. Novice runners cave to the body's demands. They're attached to themselves. Runners like Rod, they learn to let go.

Without thought, he pulled ahead of the sophomore. His legs moved, but not of his orders. The world around him vanished. The stadium, stands, crowd, track, noises, smells; his body, all melted away. There was no thought, no senses, no pain, just instinct. Rod's thoughts were now no more complex than a gazelle's, and the sophomore behind was a cheetah.

He closed in on the finish line. Each stride separated him further from his adversary. A revelation. He would win! The survival instinct rested replaced by nervous chills. Glorious chills, shivering through every atom of his core, tingled in his fingertips, radiated through his quivering legs. His arms started that magnificent journey toward the sky. Fifteen meters remained and ...

"I don't deserve it," he sputtered.

The words literally dropped from his lips. Though Newton's laws did their best not to disobey, Rod's screeching halt caused some in the stunned crowd to wonder. The sophomore blasted by on the right. Glory was his. He raised his arms and wept. Rod scoffed at the arrogance.

"You didn't win," he whispered. Then he turned to aid his ailing competitor. As the rest of the field sprinted toward the finish, Rod sprinted away. He sprinted straight to the Cuban, who lay comatose in lane three. The view from so close was disturbing.

Twisted, contorted, discolored, limp, blue, the body looked like a corpse. The Cuban's tongue drooped from his mouth, touching the track. Over 10,000 watched, but Rod felt alone. Paramedics would wait another 20 seconds until the other competitors had cleared the track. Where was instinct now?

"Hey," Rod started nervously. "Hey, you alright?" He extended his arm and shook the fallen runner. The Cuban's arm flopped to the ground, and the body rolled onto its back. The boy's eyes shifted back in his head. Rod turned and got sick in the grass.

Medics arrived. CPR commenced. Rod could never remember finishing vomiting. All he remembered was watching in horror as paramedics took turns administering mouth-to-mouth. What felt like eternity was six minutes. Then they whisked the Cuban away. Rod didn't even know his name.

Fear, shame, hope, dread, sadness, confusion, a bag of mixed emotions washed over him. Propped back on his elbows, Rod failed to notice his own vomit seeping through the butt of his shorts. Again the world around him vanished. The stadium, stands, crowd, his body, they all melted away. But this time, even instinct disappeared. The world was timeless, until a god-like voice pulled him from his trance.

"You all right?"

Coach Rollins hovered above his young prodigy. Rod said nothing. He blankly stared up at his hero. Coach extended his hand. Rod took it. So large, so strong, it pulled him up without a hint of trouble. They stood face to face. Coach's eyes teared seeing his runner's wounded expression. Clutching each other in a tight embrace, grown man and child wept freely.

Chapter II

Coach always walked with a limp. Each stride of his left leg carried a subtle hitch. A casual onlooker would struggle to see it. Even acquaintances often failed to notice the malfunction. But we knew it. When we decelerated from our warm-up runs and he'd start walking from the shelter in our direction, it was glaring. By the time we were upperclassmen, though his gait hadn't changed, we all chipped in to buy him a cane as a season-end gift.

No one knew its origin. No one dared to ask. Year after year, upperclassmen passed rumors of its starting point down to the newcomers. Four years later, they'd pass it down again. Fantastic tales developed over a quarter century. The summer prior to my senior year, the truth about coach's limp was both legend and mystery.

One story was that fresh out of college, after a disappointing career, coach went berserk. He moved to a backland cabin, started running 200-mile weeks, and briefly dominated the road racing circuit under a pseudo name.

Our research turned up an interesting character around the right time period. One Morning Dove Morris, who won several major road races. A BIX 7, Peach Tree 10K, and Carlsbad 5000 earned him national attention. That is, until he mysteriously disappeared.

We researched the Morning Dove legend to death, religiously scouring the internet, books, magazines, race registers. But nothing was conclusive. It had happened in the day before media gave running its proper attention. The pictures were too few and too grainy. Even if they hadn't been, Morning Dove's beard was so thick that we might not have recognized him as coach, even in high definition.

Another legend had coach leading the Boston Marathon at the 21st mile. He looked strong until Heartbreak Hill. The story was that up the last bump, he started to falter. His lead crumbled. The second pack gobbled him up. Forced to keep calling the race, the announcers forgot about the upstart, who'd led for so long. Once the leaders crossed the line the cameras tried to go back; but he'd disappeared. They assumed he'd crawled into the crowd, into oblivion, never to return again. Nobody knew. But I can safely say, there was an eerie resemblance in the eyes of our ancient coach and that young runner leading the race in the videotape.

School had been out for a week, and four guys from the team were wasting away the afternoon at Angeno's Pizza. As usual, the mystery became a topic of our conversation again.

"I ran by coach yesterday," I said. "The limp was out of control."

I stuffed half a slice of pizza in my mouth. Four of us chewed. This is how runner's converse when they eat.

Utter a sentence, stuff the mouth, chew. Next guy swallows, utters a response, chews. There's not much time to talk when you need to consume an extra 1,500 calories a day.

John Creighton had been along for the run. Anxious to speak, he did double time with his jaw.

"He looked flippin' terrible," he belched. "Excuse me. Looked about a hundred and fifty."

"Can you stop with the cussing?"

"I didn't cuss."

"Close enough, and what's this thing with coach that's so terrible?"

The speaker was Jeremy Sylas. He was still too young to see the limp and far too religious to appreciate the universal usefulness of certain four-letter words. Creighton smirked. The sophomore was stepping into our trap. Fourth in the State Mile, he'd fallen into coach's favor. Unbeknownst to him, he'd been dubbed "The Chosen One." He'd been chosen by his elders to be the next to ask coach about the limp.

"Whatta you mean what am I talking about? The limp. You know, the big flippin' limp."

More chewing. Sylas piously shook his head.

"Cut him some slack, Creighton," I said. "He wasn't there for the banquet. The cane?"

More chewing. Todd Busch was still working on the same bite of pizza from the start of the conversation.

"Are you saying he can't see the limp?"

"It's hard when you're young."

"If you're blind! C'mon, the guy needs a new hip."

"For heaven's sake," Sylas squealed.

"You don't even think I'm going to heaven."

"The limp's not that bad," Sylas continued. He wanted to say more, but the pizza proved too tempting.

"You just haven't been around long enough, Sylas," said Creighton. He mashed a cheesy breadstick into his mouth. Glancing in my direction, he passed the baton of conversation.

"He's right, Sylas. That leg's getting bad. And we don't even know how it got like that."

The trap was set.

"So why doesn't someone just ask him?" he stood in the snare.

"Are you kidding? Try asking your mom if she's okay with you being the head of a harem."

"He's not that scary."

"That's because you don't get pulled by yourself in the push-pull five miler."

"I work pretty hard."

"I didn't say you didn't."

A smile broke across my face. He'd taken the bait. "But if anyone's gonna ask, I say it be you. Coach loves you."

"Woah, hold on! I didn't agree ..."

"Too late," broke in Creighton. He was so anxious to speak, that he spit his breadstick into Busch's lasagna. "You're committed."

Sylas turned crimson.

"I'm not committed to anything," he screeched. "You can't make me ask ..."

"Listen, sophomore!" I screamed. My fingertip

was two inches from his face. "You don't get to make choices yet. I don't care if you are the fastest guy on the team." I glared straight into his heavenly soul. He cowered. "Furthermore, you owe us one."

As if on cue, everyone's heads simultaneously snapped in my direction. Creighton crossed his arms upon his emaciated chest. It was obvious he was displeased with my deviating from the script.

"What are you talking about, Weaver," he spit.

"He ran terrible at the State Cross Meet. It cost us three places," I said.

Surprisingly, my statement was met with general nods of approval. They were all such moderates, vulnerable to the slightest propaganda campaign. The Benedict Arnolds turned to give Sylas an evil eye. He reeled back in his chair.

"I had a fever of 101."

They turned again.

"Well ... if you hadn't gone to the football game the week before, in the freezing rain, you'd have never got sick!"

Sylas was done. Alibi slashed, he uttered some crap about how warm he'd dressed, but we all knew that attending an ogre-ball game was sinful. A skilled diplomat, he started to compromise.

"I'll make you a deal."

"No deals."

"As I recall, your State race wasn't one for the ages either." Little squirt had a point.

"What do you propose?"

He devoured a breadstick to buy himself think

time. "Tomorrow morning, we have a time trial on the track," Sylas said, pausing mid-sentence to wash down the lump of food in his throat. "You break 4:40, I ask coach about the limp. You run any slower, I'm off the hook."

Intriguing, 4:40 certainly wasn't out of reach. I'd run 4:43 twice in May. I leaned back and pondered the offer. Ethics. No doubt I could use my upper class status to force him to ask. But I'd screwed up. I'd challenged his honor by insulting his run. Now that he'd dug up my dirt, it was a question of honor. I decided to win back my pride.

"All right," I responded. My agreement was met with a roar of approval. "That's a fair deal. One stipulation though, I don't have to break 4:40, I just have to run it."

Sylas extended his hand and sealed my fate. Suddenly my plans for a hard evening 6-miler were flushed down the toilet. I'd run four easy instead. Sylas glanced down at his watch.

"I gotta go guys. Errands to run. Track at eight?"

I nodded approval. He dropped a ten and headed for the door. Three of us sat silently chewing. After the waitress dropped the bill, Creighton spoke his mind.

"What'd you make that deal for, man? You had all the negotiating power. You didn't have to give him anything."

"He had a good point," I said, my expression pained from tabulating the check. "My State race was garbage. It wasn't fair to call him out like that."

"So what if it wasn't fair. Generations have come and gone and still nobody knows the origin of the limp. This was our chance!"

I stopped for a moment, too discombobulated to attempt the arduous task of figuring the tip. Then I turned to my friend, gave him a scowl.

"There's no guarantee coach tells him anything even if he does ask. Besides, I've run pretty close to 4:40 a few times this year. I think I've got a good shot."

"As long as you're confident," Creighton snapped. "But for your sake, I sure hope you've got it. Cause if you don't, a lot of people ain't gonna be happy."

What a jerk. I dropped my share of the check and walked out without saying goodbye. That night I ran alone.

Chapter III

"Dang it!"

Rod's warm up pants were stuck on his shoe.

"Cripes."

The inside liner just couldn't quite get over the toe. He tried tugging, pulling, yanking, shaking, cussing; anything to avoid having to undo the zipper. Rip!

"Judas Iscariot!"

The holy trilogy was now complete.

The pants were up. Rod sat back on his elbows, an exasperated look on his face. A few coaches were still mulling around the field house, but for the most part it was empty. Rod marveled at its transfiguration since the morning.

Before the race, it was a cornucopia of action. Everywhere he turned, humanity was engaged in some running-related task. Runners were striding, coaches instructing, officials dictating; the State Meet atmosphere was track at its finest. The post-meet letdown was track at its worst.

A post-race nausea overwhelmed the young harrier. The old field house smelled of mildew and rubber. Only the low drone of colossal circulation fans filled the stifling June air. A stiff breeze blowing through the propped doors was all that kept the temperature under 90-degrees.

Rod's movements were ghostly, each shift of his lanky limbs as deliberate as the setting of the sun. Sweat soaked his rag of frizzy brown hair. Why had he tried to get his warm-ups on anyway?

He sat alone, his only company a plain black duffle bag. As he moped about his campsite, he looked like a victim of a shipwreck sitting on an island. Bones protruded from his gaunt body. His head bowed toward the ground in meditation. Sweat streaks stained his bony cheeks, tear streaks the bridge of his nose, passionate thoughts his mind. The image of the fallen Cuban wouldn't disappear.

A sigh rang from the pit of his stomach. This day should have been his crowning moment, the reward for 600 miles of off-season training. He'd sacrificed everything a kid could sacrifice: grades, friends, family, sleep. What had it gotten him? Nothing. All those miles, in the snow, sleet, freezing rain, bitter cold, all for naught. This moment his confidence wavered. In late February, it convinced him he couldn't lose.

He was a running machine. Oiled to perfection, his late winter runs felt effortless. For most people, the legs must be pulled forward to run. For Rod the machine ran so efficiently, that they needed pulling back. Aware of his pupil's passion for the run, Coach Rollins worked hard to save Rod from his youthful enthusiasm.

"Cut back," he'd ordered.

Rod's belief in his mentor was unflinching. Obediently, he cut his mileage. But what if he hadn't? Would the

Cuban have created such a lead?

Rod's stiff legs nearly gave way as he pushed himself up. He slung his bag across his shoulder and headed for the exit. Tranquility accompanied him along his walk. Something about the humming of the fans was comforting. At the double steel doors he stopped for a moment of contemplation.

Mixed feelings consumed him: Sadness about his loss, fear about the Cuban's health, pride in his choice to refuse such hollow victory, hope that his senior year would finally bring a title. Another year of work lay ahead, months of drudgery, oppressive heat, bitter cold, and no assurances. Rod closed his eyes and mourned lost opportunity. Then, he turned to start anew.

His first step into this new day gave him cause to believe that it was he who'd perished on the track. Hundreds of flashes blinded him. Rod shielded his eyes with a forearm. What on earth? His name was hailed from all directions.

"Mr. Dillery, what you did was unbelievable. Why did you decide to stop?"

"Mr. Dillery, Mr. Dillery. Did you know how bad your opponent's condition was?" Rod cautiously lowered his shield. Countless reporters drooled like starving wolves. Evening loomed, and they were in a desperate rush to beat their deadlines. Oblivious to Rod's fragile mindset, they hurled callus questions. The boy stood speechless, mouth agape, eyes hunting for a familiar face. A feeling of claustrophobia overwhelmed him. He frantically began pushing his way through the horde. His violent, shoves knocked several reporters to the floor. This made them hungrier.

Rod's universe transformed to a blur. Trapped within the sea of suits and cameras, the flashes were like lightning and the howls as deafening as a Harley revving at a stoplight. A feeling of apprehension built up exponentially. He wanted out; he needed out. If escape eluded him, so would sanity.

Sweat gushed from his pores. He felt faint, suffocated, trapped. In every direction they harassed him. They grabbed him and pushed microphones in his face. A swirl of mouths yammered up and down, voices meshing into an incoherent vernacular.

"I don't deserve this. What I did was good," he thought.

"Let me out," he whispered. "Let me out. For the love of heaven let me go!"

The last words were a scream.

But the story was too juicy. A young man gives up a State title to help an opponent in need. Headlines like that don't present themselves on demand. The reporters were a savvy bunch. So they tightened the noose, sealing every nook and hole through which Rod could possibly escape. They tormented him like children do a cranky uncle. They prodded him to speak. He tried to walk away, but they wouldn't let him.

Down the sidewalk, through the maze of traffic exiting the parking lot, they accompanied him. Finally, he reached his little red Chevy, and they could follow him no further. So they blocked his path. Every direction he turned, there was a talking head.

"Were you friends with the boy, Mr. Dillery?"

"Are you disappointed in losing the State Championship?"

"Have you heard anything about his status?"

Rod couldn't take much more. He balled his fists. Dark minions murdered his conscience. A scowl enveloped his face. Sin penetrated his heart. A punch was coming. A fist cocked back. The crowd gasped. Then, just in time to prevent the assault, a familiar voice thundered through the dusk air.

"Leave the boy alone," roared Coach Rollins. "He doesn't want to hear your questions. You saw what happened! Just write your story and leave him be!"

The throng fell silent. Rollins stared them down. Rod stood slack-jawed. A minute passed. Then, one by one, the reporters started to walk away. Slamming car doors and revving engines filled the crisp, evening air. Coach stood stoically, arms folded sternly across his chest until every last one of them was gone. He turned to face his pupil. Rod felt that fearful love all boys have of their father.

"You ran well," coach said.

Rod bowed his head.

"You ran well enough to win."

Rod grimaced with disappointment.

"Hold your head up."

The young harrier slowly looked up into his coach's eyes.

"Even if you hadn't stopped you wouldn't be satisfied. If you want it," Coach paused deliberately. Rod waited anxiously for more. "Earn it."

Coach walked away. Rod followed him with his

eyes all the way to the car. The door slammed, the engine revved, and coach drove out of the lot. Rod watched the car drive up County Road 30 and turn right on highway 12. Silence.

"Earn it."

Rod stared into the distance. He saw Limestone Hill standing at the center of Elm Creek Park Reserve. Home was on the other side, about 12 miles away. He jangled the car keys in his hand.

"Earn it."

He looked down at his running shoes.

The red Chevy spent the night alone.

Chapter IV

Rigor-mortis-legs: **n.** A condition afflicting distance runners before 8:00 A.M. in which the muscles below the waist stiffen, inhibiting range of motion upwards of 40%. Man I was groggy. No high school kid should have to get up before eight during the summer. Yet there I was, thrashing through the puddles of a late June shower. My watch read 7:35. My rigor-mortis-legs made a 4:40 mile feel more distant than the edge of infinity.

The rain made my shoes feel like lead. Each step added water weight. Each ounce would add seconds. I already had a three second handicap, so the rain was a psychological disaster.

Seeing the light towers of Osseo's football field did nothing to ease my trepidation. Panic nested itself deep beneath my saturated skin. My nerves tingled. The hairs of my arms rose with apprehension. Nausea crawled up my scratchy throat. The track got closer. What I saw made me squint.

It was not what I expected. It was not the picturesque scene of a lonely track, waking on a dreary morning. A large crowd was gathered. They came for blood. They came to witness my suffering. Gloomily, I trotted to the fence. Creighton addressed me cheerily.

"I thought I'd give you some added inspiration by rounding up a few old friends."

He'd nearly inspired me to turn around. I skewered him with a glare.

"What's the matter chap? Too many supporters?"

A circle of bodies three thick engulfed me. The whole team: Busch, Markson, Johnson, Lyle, Longley, Murry, Tyson, all 21 of them. And some specially selected hotties from the women's team that Creighton had lured out of bed with the promise of free Dunkin' Doughnuts. My guardian angel was among them.

Her name was Carrie Amundson. She'd been the target of my sheepish stares since the first day of practice freshman year. As always, she looked gorgeous. She had long black hair, a petite runner's body, and a chest that filled out a jog bra with shocking fullness.

My sole desire was to kiss her just once before we graduated. It was an innocent crush. There are the girls you visualize during alone time and there are the girls you're too ashamed to even fantasize about. She was the latter. Her mere presence had made me temporarily oblivious to the morning's events. Creighton's voice brought me back into reality.

"I've got one more surprise, too," my tormenter chuckled. "Take a look behind."

Slowly I turned, dreading what I'd see.

"Good heavens," I exclaimed. "You ... you ... why the heck did you invite Coach?"

Creighton sneered. "So when you break 4:40, Sylas

won't have time to compromise his way out again."

I'd have smacked him if my arms weren't the size of pipe cleaners. I'd have called him names unfit for print had coach not walked up and slapped me on the back.

"So I hear you're going to run 4:40," he proclaimed, a childlike giddiness in his voice. "I'm looking forward to it. But you'd better start soon, this weather's looking nasty."

I gingerly plopped into a hurdler stretch. My desperate attempts to regain the elasticity I'd lost in the night were proving highly ineffective. The tension of the situation did nothing to help. How embarrassing. If I didn't break 4:40 now, I'd never live it down. And in front of Carrie to boot. Whew, she looked good, so good I had to stretch my hamstrings extra time, to hide the signs of my adolescence.

Despite coach's prodding, I wasn't in a hurry. Let them soak. Muffled grumbling gained momentum with each newly invented stretch I tried. I might have listened if Carrie weren't there, but I was too enamored. Every chance I got, I took a peak at her beautiful face, sultry lips, curvaceous, ...

"You ready yet!" screamed Creighton. "You stopped lacing your shoes a minute ago. Stop staring at Amundson and do your strides."

The next time we were alone, I'd slit his throat. It'd have been one thing to embarrass me away from the presence of a goddess, but by making the comment in front of her, Creighton twisted an arrow buried deep within my flesh. I was too ashamed to look in her direction.

"Start your strides!"

I bounded sheepishly from my seat and did a stride halfway around the track. My legs felt extraordinary. Midway down the backstretch, I decelerated into a gentle trot.

"Focus," I whispered.

Nervous butterflies started tickling my throat. The thought of the pain I'd soon endure was enough to cause my right leg to momentarily give out. There was a stumble but no fall. It was time to stride the other way.

I marveled at the crispness of my limbs. Perhaps two weeks away from coach's training was what I needed for rejuvenation. By the time I hit the straightaway, I was sprinting faster than I ever had. Momentum carried me a solid 50 meters further than I intended. A slow trot back to the start and I was ready.

"Let's do this," I shouted. "Who's timing?"

"You want a rabbit?" asked Creighton.

"He doesn't get a rabbit," Sylas furiously interjected. "This isn't the Olympics. Either the man can run 4:40 or he can't."

Creighton turned to coach.

"What do you think, coach? Normally he'd have people to race with, why can't he have some help here?"

Coach took a second to formulate his response. Whether intentionally or not, he answered in support of his favorite runner.

"I think he ought to do it on his own accord. If he can do it that way, then we know he's one tough cookie."

The mist was so cold I couldn't have cared less one way or the other.

"Can I just run, please? I don't really care."

"Get on the line," responded coach. "I'll keep the time, if nobody objects."

As if anyone would tell God no.

Anxiously, I ambled up to the stripe. I hated these last few seconds. I loathed competition, to the point of trying to sprain my ankle off of a curb before big races. It just gave me this sick paralyzing feeling in my lower spine. It wouldn't go away for at least 300 meters.

Coach gave the readying command. I leaned forward. Then he launched me off, with his chillingly familiar practice start.

"Ready ...."

Good grief the pause was long.

"Goooooooooooooooooo!"

My legs exploded off the teardrop and into turn one and the start command drowned in the pitter patter of the rain. The queasiness intensified and spread; my spine went weak. Were the feeling not a familiar one, I'd have worried about the possibility of my legs giving way. But I knew better. By 300 meters the sick feeling would be history. The only downside was that it would be replaced by an even more discouraging first twinge of pain.

Lap one passed quickly. As I approached the straightaway, the first signs of fatigue materialized: faster breathing, arms tightening in on the chest, cold sweats. My body had begun the rapid downward spiral from minor discomfort to untainted suffering. It was all part of the plan. If I wanted to break 4:40, by 600 meters I knew I needed to be in a state of self-inflicted asphyxiation.

The straightaway passed quickly, without incident. My confidence swelled. I even took a millisecond to observe Carrie. Her gaze was intense. She almost looked impressed.

"Sixty-eight," thundered coach.

This was a welcome surprise. Sixty-eight had never felt this comfortable. Something clicked. Recklessly, I increased tempo. Memories of coach yelling at us from the bike at the end of wicked interval sessions filled my mind.

"Short and quick. Get that tempo up!"

The risk didn't come without punishment. My lungs revolted. All pathways in and out constricted. Goopy saliva cloaked my throat. I hacked up gobs of mucus with violent coughs. Blood gurgled up from my esophagus. The race was on.

Fearlessly, I plowed through the 600-mark. A cheating glance at my watch. The split was obnoxious. Or were my computation skills too severely compromised? What did it matter? Fast or not, the question was whether I was willing to take a risk.

"I will," I decided. "Today I can die!"

Lactic acid scorched my quads. My eyes raged with the fury of Satan. I grimaced, focused forward, my only goal in life to live until the next straight. My past limitations faded. At 800-meters I saw the awe upon the faces of the mass. Coach bellowed the sizzling time.

"2:17! Short and quick! Don't let up!"

I ran past their screams so fast that the sound barely reached my ears. My body was in frantic need of fuel. It felt like I was suffocating. My limbs and chest contracted inward. My legs were burning. Every instinct forced my body to resist the forward movement. All I wanted was to lie down in the grass and die.

"He's fading." Creighton announced on the opposite side of the track. Coach unleashed a booming yell.

"Let it hurt, Curt Weaver!"

Most race encouragement is tossed aside like dirty underwear. People remind you what you need to do with grating wails. For an instant you remember. Perhaps you loosen up the arms, relax the face, or focus on a more efficient stride. But once they're out of sight, they're out of mind. Pain clouds the memory. And you forget.

But for some reason, coach's yell resonated through my mind and wouldn't leave. I grappled against the tightness with all my might. I shook loose my arms. Usually this practice heralded my demise. Not today. Today the shackles buckled. My body was free.

My limbs loosened up dramatically. A second wind allowed them to turn with unrestrained velocity. More efficient, my body reduced its demands for oxygen. I careened around the curve and into the straightaway. Five hundred meters remained, and I was in a full tilt sprint.

"3:29," bellowed coach, as I entered into the bell lap. All I needed now was a 71. Every motivational phrase I'd ever heard cluttered up my head.

"Faster you run, the sooner you're done! It's supposed to hurt! Suffering is the sole origin of consciousness."

For an instant, I thought I might finish with a 61-second quarter. Then, around the turn, a side stitch pierced my liver. It should have ended there. But I kept running. And there was the key. In spite of every obstacle, I kept putting one foot ahead of the other.

Later, I'd compare the feeling to passing my first stone. But I kept running. Acid bubbled up and burned my throat. I kept running. Delirium made my body weave. I kept running. Pain became my only connection to existence. I still kept running.

One step at a time, right foot, left foot, breathe. Getting ample air was impossible. It felt like I was underwater but couldn't reach the surface. I prepared for the shame of dropping to my knees. Then, out of nowhere, the finish line appeared. I still have no recollection of the previous 200 meters. I just remember taking one step at a time. Finish in sight, inspiration now carried me home.

My short stride transformed to a lightning chop. The world moved in slow motion. I could see my friends waving and cheering, but it took eternity for their hands to rise. Their roar could be heard for miles, but to me it sounded jumbled and illogical. Senses cloudy, pain ripping at every pore, I craved only to be done.

"Please, God, let me finish! Let it end! I'll never run again!"

Time seemed to stop. My senses went numb. My thoughts were a scrambled, useless mush. At some point along the way I crossed the line. My next memory was being doubled over on the rubber surface of the track, emptying my stomach. A watch appeared in the stream of blood.

"Four thirty-seven," Creighton screamed. "Look at the watch, Weaver! Four thirty-seven."

Next, coach bent over.

"That was one tough run," he complimented, "I'll be expecting 4:30 by spring."

Between gags, I managed a hint of a smile. Then, I flopped over on my side and did everything in my power to ignore the annoying pleas to get up off the ground. Everyone's an expert on recovery when they aren't the ones ingesting regurgitated breakfast. This particular congregation, felt particularly compelled to grace me with their depth of knowledge.

"Stand up, you'll breathe better."

"Move around. It speeds recovery."

"If you don't get in a cool down, you'll be sore tomorrow."

Tomorrow seemed a million years away. What did I care if I was sore? I'd promised myself that I'd never run again! Screw them. I could drown in lactic soreness for all I cared. However, even the most independent soul is a slave to someone.

"Get up."

"Crap," I mumbled.

"Get up, I said." It was coach's voice.

I staggered to my feet and feebly rested in Creighton's arms. He nearly blew my eardrums with a scream.

"Sylas!"

"I know! I know! Give a man a minute for heaven's sake!"

"Was that a cuss?"

"No!"

Sylas paced along the start line, looking pale and worried. He had the air of a man unable to propose. Creighton finally forced his hand.

"It's time, Sylas!"

Resigned to his unlucky fate, Sylas started jogging

in the direction of coach's truck. We all watched as the lanky sophomore caught coach from behind and tapped him on the shoulder.

"Oh, mercy."

My stomach cramps returned. I witnessed no more of the conversation. When it was over, Sylas recollected how it went.

"Coach! Hold on a second," he called, stopping the king in his tracks. Coach may have left a lesser runner coughing in a trail of exhaust, but he was too enamored with Sylas' talent to let a chance to mentor him pass.

"What can I do for you, Jeremy?"

"Well," Sylas muddled. "The guys and I have a question about something ..." he paused to find the right phrase.

"And?"

"Well, I don't quite know how to say this, but we've noticed that you've got a, um, a limp."

Sylas felt the burden of the world lift from his shoulders.

"And we were just kind of curious about how you got it."

Coach chuckled good-naturedly. Comforted by coach's indifference to the question, Sylas chuckled with him.

"Another generation, another great runner forced to ask the question."

Sylas was shocked by the revelation; he'd not expected this.

"They always ask about the limp."

Coach stared into Sylas pale blue eyes. The sophomore started trembling.

"It's not much of a story really. I don't know why you're all so interested."

Sylas licked his lips. Perplexed looks rained down on him from the track. All the while, coach rambled.

"You know who you really ought to ask? Do you know?"

"Uh, no."

"You ought to ask the team from 1968. They knew firsthand. Idiots didn't bother to pass down the information. I suppose it shouldn't surprise me."

"Why is that?"

"That group had a grade point average of about three point three."

"It's not four point, but that's not exactly bad."

"Combined!"

Sylas understood.

"Anyway," coach continued in a voice as soothing as a tranquilizer. "You want to know about the limp. You want to know why I've got this hitch. You see me running along in the park and wonder what's wrong with me, don't you? You all wonder why I don't run with you guys."

The tone of the conversation didn't sound good. One, it looked like finding out about the limp wasn't going to happen. Two, coach was babbling on like a psychopath.

"I'll make you a deal."

Sylas' ears tuned in. He'd nearly fallen asleep standing up, listening to the coach drag on.

"Well," raved the loony. "Do you want to make a deal?"

"Yeah, sure!"

"Here's the deal. You win a State Championship this fall, I tell you how I got the limp."

Before the words had exited his mouth, coach entered his vehicle and slammed the door. The engine revved, coach put the truck in drive, and Sylas was left watching the old Ford Ranger drive out of the junior high parking lot. A curious crowd probed him for information when he arrived back on the track. Gentle rain pattered all around but nobody left until he told us what had happened.

"You're full of it," Creighton scolded. "You're telling me he said he'll only tell you if you win State."

"That's what he said."

Still reeling from the torture of the time trial, my body winced reflexively.

"So you're telling me I just ran that for nothing?"

"Not nothing. All I've got to do is win State."

Creighton scoffed at Sylas' comment.

"All you have to do, all you have to do," the volume of his voice rising considerably with the repetition.

"You're good, Sylas, but winning State? C'mon."

"I was fourth in the mile."

"Fifth if that guy didn't go down," I reminded him.

"Only two of them are back."

"You were 18th in cross, remember. How many of them were back?"

Sylas paid no heed to my lack of confidence. He just stood silently. It was at this moment that I first thought Sylas had the look of a champion. It was something in his eye, a penetrating stare, an air of confidence that just says, "ain't nobody on this planet who can beat me." Though Creighton continued to badger the sophomore, I felt inclined to stop.

"I don't know what you said to him down there, but you've got to ask him in front of us. We need witnesses."

"No way, Creighton," Sylas protested. "I held up my end of the deal. I'm even willing to put in some extra work to make it happen."

"Don't give me that crap," the scrappy senior ranted. But Sylas's aura truly shone now. Cracking a smile in my direction, he paid me my captain's tribute. It was as if he knew what I was thinking. I could sense by the posture of some others that they saw the change in Sylas too. Then he paid Creighton the ultimate disrespect, cutting him off mid-sentence.

"Tomorrow you're going to ..."

"Weaver, will you make sure my stuff gets home if I go for a run?"

"Huh, sure." Sylas stripped off his warm-ups to the loud remonstrations of Creighton.

"You slimy little son of a .... You don't talk to a senior like that."

Sylas flipped his pants to the feet of his aggressor.

"See you around, Creighton," he said. Then he turned and ran away. Creighton didn't take kindly to the embarrassment.

"Let's go, Carrie," he grumbled angrily. Without a word to anyone else, he walked to the car.

Amused by the disrespect paid to my overzealous friend, I smiled. Far in the distance I could see Sylas pounding away up Limestone Hill.

    "He just might do it guys," I said. "He just might do it."

Chapter V

Elm Creek Park was an emerald in the midst of suburban sprawl. Slightly elevated, it flourished in Minnesota's rains while less fortunate marshlands suffocated down below. It was a steamy July evening, and Rod burst through the park boundary at a clip better than six minutes per mile.

Limestone hill loomed ahead. It'd been two weeks since Rod had hammered the 12 miles home from the State Meet. He'd run up that hill 47 times since that night, at least three times each day.

The hill's dominant feature was a steep, semi-paved utility trail running parallel to the main road. Exactly 1.5 miles from home, its beginning was where every run officially started. Rod didn't even bother to log the warm up. About a half mile in, the trail split left, away from the road and into the wilderness. From there it was about 600 meters up to Limestone Point, the highest spot in Hennepin County.

Rod loved that spot more than any place else in the world. All runners have a special place, a place where soreness dissipates, strains mend, and the mind relaxes.

Here, atop the land of ten thousand lakes, was Rod's spot. Amid the lush grasses of the hilltop, he felt at one with nature. From his lofty vantage he could see the entire world below.

Rod's feet crunched the gravel of the trail. It was time to go. The acceleration started slowly. Form was his focus; he concentrated on loosening up his shoulders. Every hundred meters or so, he edged the pace up modestly. By the time the trail forked off the road, he was hammering up the hill at under 5:30 a mile.

His breathing hit a steady rhythm. An internal pendulum tracked the pace of his legs. Steady as a car on cruise it went: one, two, three, four, one, two, three, four. Occasionally his tongue would poke between dry lips, but otherwise his movements never wavered.

Nirvana for a runner is the point at which the body finds its rhythm in combination with an intense state of relaxation. For Rod the moment had arrived. As he crested the hilltop, he transcended his existence. Cut off from ill thoughts, his senses scanned the beautiful view before him, interpreting it mystically rather than in words.

A massive marshland lay before him. Cool air rushed up the hillside pushing the daytime heat away. Steamy mist twisted around the treetops. The forest looked as if on fire without the flames.

The trail split again. Each step became progressively more inhospitable. Rod instinctively veered left, toward the more challenging portion. Thick foliage lining the edge of this spur wouldn't allow for shortcuts. Choosing this fork condemned Rod to 14-miles miles of hardship.

Rod crashed down the backside of the hill. He hurtled through snarled grasses and tore around treacherous bends, paying caution no respect. Crackling and crunching, each footstep played a beat of a great symphony. The song was a constant reminder of the importance of unrelenting tempo.

To assure victory in next year's State Meet, Rod knew he must train without boundaries. He must defy the risk of injury, spit in the face of over-training, and risk everything. It would be an excruciating journey. His body would rebel. Soreness would never leave him. His legs would ache, his bowels would grumble, and his mind would constantly be fried. It was a journey that wouldn't end until he victoriously broke the tape of the State Cross Country finish, or died trying.

He visualized the race with religious fervor. Each run he pictured himself crashing through the tape. He would sprint 30 meters past the line, bury every meter, and ignore the screams of officials. Only after passing through the chute in its entirety, would he turn to measure his dominance. Each time he turned around, he saw no one. The second runner hadn't even turned out of the woods, 300 meters behind.

These thoughts served as fuel for Rod as he thrashed through the thick patches of foliage. Spurred on by adrenaline, he red-lined the tempo to five minutes per mile. The sun was setting in the west. Dusk warned of darkness within the hour.

"Let it come," Rod shouted. "Bring it on! I'll run until the sun comes up again!"

Droplets of sweat sprayed off his body. Droplets of

mist replaced them. His heart hammered on his sternum. His lungs expanded to unimaginable proportions. Defying nature's rules, his legs ate up the acid trying to slow them down. Rod was a machine! No, not yet! He was becoming a machine. Each day must be like this. Each day he must run with this wild intensity.

"Pay no heed to aches and pains, they'll heal," he thought. "You're young. You are invincible!"

Such unflappable confidence virtually assured him victory. His goals moved clearly into view. Nothing in the world could strike him down.

"Nothing!"

And then, out of nowhere, the Slayer materialized. Like a phantom from the depths of Hades, he came charging from the shadows of the mist. Clad in orange, he thrust forward at a terrifying pace. He stared at Rod with malice. Their eyes locked. Both harriers knew what was at stake. Both knew they had a capable rival. With only one spot at the top of the podium, both knew they must risk everything to win.

Rod could physically feel the tension as they passed each other by. And then he was alone. His nostrils flared with rage. Now his task was truly daunting. This orange warrior who'd passed him was no slouch. He'd run in the State Mile two weeks before. Rod wasn't sure, but he believed the Osseo High runner had finished in the top five.

He was irritated. Irritated by his laziness over the past couple of weeks. Why hadn't he trained more? Why hadn't he trained harder? He'd logged only 120 miles those first two weeks. Now he was at a disadvantage. He was sure of it.

Only one method exists for closing such a training gap. Rod would simply have to run longer and harder than his foe. He exhaled deeply. He scrunched his lip up to his nostrils. The last seven miles would be the test. How much suffering could he endure?

History would testify that somewhere along that seven-mile trail, Rod Dillery made the choice. All elite runners come to a crossroads in their career where they are faced with such a decision. On some run, far from home, distant from all humanity, a revelation occurs.

"I have a choice. I can run timid, ensure my health and have a happy productive but unspectacular career. I can be ordinary. Or, I can push the envelope. I can run three times a day, at a blistering pace, in sweltering heat or mind numbing cold. I can defy those who tell me I'll get hurt or burn out and increase the intensity of my training. I can choose to take the risk that my sacrifice will be in vain. And in taking that risk, I can become a running god."

Out of the darkness, Rod stepped in the door of his house. Tense muscles cramped with every movement. Off went the clothes to the floor and he hobbled straight to the shower. Ten-minutes later he slogged naked from the bathroom to bed. He collapsed, too exhausted to clothe himself.

His mother and father were accustomed to the silence of their boy. Usually they paid no notice to the way he dragged around. But that night Mrs. Dillery saw a difference in her son. She wasn't sure what it was, but before she went to sleep she made mention of it to her husband.

"Did you see Rod come in tonight, Tom?" Her voice quivered with uneasy trepidation. Mr. Dillery groaned. He was already asleep, and his wife's voice tortured his ears.

"Ugggghh, nahh, I didn't catch him," he mumbled. He cleared his throat and continued. "He ran an hour past dark, I was already asleep by the time he came in. Don't worry 'bout ..."

Back to sleep he went. Despite his advise, she worried.

"Tom, he looked awful. He was having trouble getting undressed for the shower. I just don't want him to hurt himself."

Mr. Dillery snored. He was oblivious to his wife's observation. But later on he'd bear witness to what she said. Rod Dillery was possessed. During those fateful seven miles he made his choice. He would win at all costs, even if it cost him everything.

He ran morning, noon and night, a slave to an unchanging, cruel routine. Each morning at 5:35 his alarm would screech.

"Already?!"

He was too tired.

The choppy terrain of Elm Creek Park was etched so deeply on his brain that even darkness proved no match on those cool misty mornings. He took full advantage of the brisk temperature. The first three miles were used to jog the stiffness from his legs; the last ten were used to hammer them into submission. Only submissive legs won championships.

By noon, the scorching summer sun was enough to cause birds to fall dead from the sky. But having returned home, eaten a massive bowl of oatmeal, and hydrated all morning, Rod slipped on his shoes and ran again. Only on the weekdays though, only while mom was at work. She'd worry too much if she saw how much he ran. He always claimed his morning runs were a third of what they were. She needn't know the mileage he put in. She needn't see the sacrifice.

These noon runs were a test of mental fortitude. The soaring temperature made hard running impossible. So Rod usually settled on an easy four. In spite of the relaxed tempo, these runs served a vital purpose. They exercised the mind. They simulated race conditions, forcing him to focus on relaxation. Coach always said training the mind was more important than training the body; Rod obeyed his command.

By 12:30, body depleted of all energy stores, Rod would slump over the stove and cook his noodles. Burning calories faster than the sun would a gallon of gas, he ravenously devoured all food available. Portions of noodles intended for families, slid down his throat with the consistency of well-run miles. While he waited for water to boil, he'd empty the cupboards of their stores.

Everything was a target: pickles, cheese, lunch meat, fruit, ice cream, cookies, bread, butter, crackers, bread sticks, leftover ham, chocolate, the list went on and on. The furnace continued to burn. Grocery bills continued to rise. Mrs. Dillery marveled at ferocity with which her son consumed food. Bi-weekly shopping trips became weekly, and then they happened every five days. And yet he didn't gain weight. How was this possible?

It was possible because in the evening Rod Dillery ran again. He'd rise from his afternoon nap, slap on his soaking singlet, and drag himself out the door. It didn't matter that he'd already logged 17 miles. To be champion, he needed to outwork everyone.

Back to Elm Creek he went, up the utility road, down the left trail. It was all he did. And yet, it was never enough. For no matter how much he ran, the phantom in the orange jersey was running too.

"How does he run so much," Dillery raged, each time they had a chance encounter. "How can he train more than me?"

And then he'd increase the tempo even more. Each day this pattern continued. Possessed by a fear of losing, Rod Dillery murdered caution and abused his body.

One day in early August, Tom Dillery witnessed his son's possession. In a moment of absent-mindedness his son had left his running log on the kitchen counter. A former runner himself, the senior Dillery couldn't fathom what he saw. He took the log and brought the novel-thick booklet to his wife.

"What's this?" she asked curiously.

"You were right," he said penitently. "He's possessed."

Mrs. Dillery sat down. She nearly fainted when she saw the mileage total on the last page.

"He's only been out of school nine weeks."

She did the math over and over as she stared at the page.

August 10: 13 mile morning grinder. Felt sore, I'm always sore. 4 mile nooner. Hot, but good focus. 14-mile night long run. Tired. Hungry near the end. Need a lot of noodles tonight.

Daily total: 31 Summer total: 1512

Training is principally an act of faith. Believe.

Chapter VI

It'd been a week since my triumphant time trial. Jeremy Sylas and I meandered through air-conditioned corridors of Glendale Shopping Center. Outside, the weather was hot, nearly 100 degrees. Sweat stained the shirts of larger individuals whom made the mistake of wearing blue or gray.

"Looks like the AC is having trouble keeping up," Sylas commented as a particularly large woman labored by. My mind was in other places.

"You run yet today?" I asked, hoping to find a trail partner to pull me through the heat wave.

"Yeah, I went out this morning."

Shot down. I resigned myself to a miserable night alone.

"But I felt pretty good. I'll go with you if you want."

"I'm going long," I warned.

Sylas smirked.

"How long?" he chuckled.

"Ten," I declared.

"Ten's fine."

No hesitation. His voice didn't waver. No indication of being the least bit phased by the distance. Suddenly my choice to run long didn't seem so impressive. After all, this would be Sylas' second run of the day. Maybe his first one was short.

"You sure you want to run twice?"

"Yeah, it's fine ... I didn't go too hard."

This scared me. Even without a morning run, ten seemed daunting. I would have fretted further, but we dipped into Games by James and suddenly I found myself distracted by the behemoth war-game section. Sylas shelled out $40 for the newest version of Axis and Allies. We spent the rest of the day at his house, battling in the trenches of Western Europe. It wasn't until six, that he asked the dreaded question.

"You ready to run?"

"It's still pretty hot."

"You're stalling."

I was. The thought of braving the black asphalt put a shiver in my spine.

"Stop worrying," he encouraged. "You'll be fine."

Ten minutes later we opened the front door of the house. My skin turned to leather. The heat blast scoffed at my fortitude. The humidity formed a film on my skin as we stretched on the porch. It didn't seem to bother Sylas. I marveled at his calm demeanor. I marveled at the muscles in his legs.

"You think we should go a little shorter?" I asked.

"Weaver, if you want to win State Meets, you've gotta go long on nights like these."

How embarrassing. A sophomore was telling a

senior how to train. I bowed my head in shame and kicked myself for being such a coward.

Shortly after, we began the jog toward Elm Creek Park. My formless limbs tingled with fear. Fortunately for my feeble body, Sylas seemed content to let me set the pace on the road to the nature reserve.

July's heat sizzled. I savored every second of my control. A short time later, Limestone Hill loomed on the opposite side of the park. It cast its ominous shadow upon us. Though it shielded us from the sun, we knew better than to give thanks. Patiently awaiting our arrival, it lay like a serpent, readying itself to strike. Its steep sides were venom.

We cut off the road and bushwhacked thirty meters to a thin dirt trail. A dense canopy of trees shaded the narrow strip. Nature had booby-trapped it with roots and knots. Pavement plodders despised these minor annoyances. They preferred to keep to an extensive network of bike trials in the western end of the park. Our existence on the east side was a lonely one. Sylas started edging up the pace. A shot of adrenaline went through my legs. I no longer had control.

We galloped through the forest at a sizzling sub-six minutes per mile. Limestone Hill approached with ferocious rapidity. I swallowed ruefully. Only three miles in, the three-meter gap that had separated us, grew to nearly ten. I'd spent the whole run fighting to keep up, and now I realized we were just getting started.

Sharp branches tore at my face. Jagged rocks struck at my feet. They nearly toppled me on several occasions, but my ankles rebounded with remarkable resiliency. All the while, Sylas bounded ahead of me with gazelle-like grace.

His head didn't bob an inch. Born remarkably efficient, his new training regimen solidified already meticulous form. When a log blocked his path, his legs spilt like a gymnast's, allowing him ample clearance. This same log acted like a steeple barrier for me. I was forced to plant my foot on the top of the wood, losing precious meters each time we encountered such an obstacle. By the time we arrived at the base of Limestone Hill, I was a wreck.

Then something terrible happened. Far off in the distance, a runner wearing green appeared. Though the gap between Sylas and I had been growing progressively wider, I was still close enough to hear him the moment the lonely figure barreled across the crest of the hill.

"Park Center .... I hate that ... Agggghhh!"

He'd almost cussed. I'd never seen him mad. It seemed that Sylas had come across the lonely harrier before. His sudden thrust confirmed it. I hadn't been embarrassed this badly since my brother, five years my senior, raced me years before. I would watch their encounter from a distance.

The tension wafted downwind. A cloud of ill feelings encircled me. Their eyes dueled. Searing with hatred, their retinas boiled from the whites. Obsessed with victory, each combatant sized up his opponent, supremely confident in his own superiority. Both runners accelerated recklessly. Neither was intimidated. I was the only one who was scared.

Neither looked back after passing the other. It

was time to focus inward. Unconcerned with a sloth-like creature such as myself, the mysterious runner gave no indication of even seeing me on the trail. His elbow glanced heavily against my left arm.

"Hey!"

I was too tired to say anything more. My efforts returned to keeping Sylas in sight.

It was foolish to have wasted energy thinking about the Park Center runner's rudeness. Sylas had already doubled his lead. I moaned despondently as he disappeared over the hill.

My lungs burned. The sweat in my armpits caused fresh chafing to sting. I couldn't decide which was worse, the stuffy air in my lungs or my raw salty skin. A cramp bit my calf. The first pangs of dehydration arrived. My mind broke. My pace slowed to a crawl.

My dispirited body shuffled over the hilltop, just in time to see Sylas glide away gracefully in the distance. I now faced the dangers of the heat alone. At least I could control the tempo on my own accord. Geezer trot isn't nearly as shameful when you're by yourself. I abruptly changed my heading and aimed myself for the nearest water fountain.

Dreamily, I suffered through the boggy quagmire of swampy reeds and lush leafy trees. I marveled at Sylas' transition into a running god. If I was in 4:37 shape, then he was well under 4:10.

Time became an aberration. I'm not sure how long it was before the beautiful oasis revealed itself ahead of me. All I know is that it felt like heaven when I unleashed the valve and let the icy water cool my boiling core. On a hot day, water is like a runner's cocaine; hopelessly addictive. I spent at least ten minutes soaking my head by drenching my shirt and wringing it out above me.

Only once I was thoroughly saturated, did I dare venture away from the fountain. The next forty minutes were spent slowly trudging out of the park. I don't think I'd ever been so happy just to walk. The woods cast a dark shadow over me, as the sun set low in the sky. The scent of the late blooming flowers filled my nose. All the details of God's creation came to life.

The branches of the weeping willow trees hung like mops of hair, creating a canopy across the gravel trail. Yellow roses and purple flax swayed gently in the soft summer breeze. My feet barely left the ground as they crunched the gravel. It was a perfect running surface. In this case a walking surface. Noise from behind indicated the presence of another runner coming. I shifted left to let him pass.

"What'ya walking for!"

I stopped on a dime.

"Don't just stand there, dummy! If you want to win this fall get started running."

My limbs were petrified with heat exhaustion. I feebly started trotting. Ten steps later I was throwing up. Sylas felt guilty for forcing me on.

"I'm sorry Weaver. You all right?"

"Auuuuugggggghhhhhhh!"

Cramps and knots punched my stomach and forced a second ejection.

"Auuuuuugggggghhhhhaacckkkkkaaa make it stop!"

Only the stomach lining remained. I rolled over on my side and hacked out tons of nothing. Sylas stretched silently. Oblivious to my pain, he gazed into the night sky with a contemplative air. Between hacks, I asked him what was on his mind.

"What's got you so quiet Sylas?"

He didn't move, or interrupt his stretch. He was quiet long enough that I thought he didn't hear me. I spit out a bit of phlegm and was about to ask again, when he started speaking in a thoughtful tone.

"I was thinking about that runner we passed," he said. "I think he was in the State Mile this year."

"Did you beat 'em?"

"I think. I don't remember."

A pause.

"He scares me. I've never been scared of anyone in running. But this guy ..."

"Don't worry, Sylas, ain't nobody gonna beat you."

"That's what I thought until I started this training. I've been pounding. But I swear every run I do I see that doorknob."

"Can you please cuss? I think I heard you cuss."

Sylas smiled but didn't break the second commandment.

My exhausted frame lay sprawled out across the dewy grass. I started counting the stars; it seemed more sensible than trying to comprehend the kind of training Sylas was probably doing. What kind of mileage was he doing? I mustered up the courage to ask.

"C'mon, Weaver, you know it's not ..."

"The miles it's the man," I finished.

"Screw the catch phrase, Sylas. Miles matter. How many did'ya do today?"

"Twenty."

I soiled myself.

"What about this week?"

Sylas tried to avoid answering the question.

"C'mon Weaver, let it be. You know it doesn't matter."

"How many?"

I could tell he didn't want to say it.

"A hundred thirty. But just this week!"

Everything was still. Curiosity satisfied, I felt no need to ask the dreaded next question; how many miles this summer? One look at his v-8 frame answered that. I just stood there feeling naked. My 200 miles over the past six weeks were an embarrassment.

"Just this week," I sputtered.

"Just this week. I wanted to see what I could handle."

I took his word for it. Beyond weary, my mind was in no condition to recall much about the slow final mile home. I remember Sylas was kind enough to plod along side me. And I vaguely remember my mom leading me to the sofa, placing cool rags across my head.

Suddenly it was morning. Pounding from dehydration, the vessels in my head wrapped around my brain like a boa constrictor. My dry throat forced me to the sink for water. I chugged down glass after cool glass of H_2O. Movement outside the dark window caught my attention. What I saw streaking in the dawn dumbfounded me.

First I thought it a mirage. Then, as the gray silhouette continued to fly down the lonely avenue, the form became familiar. My water glass dropped to the floor and shattered. Mere hours since our last excursion, Jeremy Sylas had found the road again. I believed.

Chapter VII

Rod's summer days were purely devoted to running. Each morning began at 5:30 when he'd cuss out his alarm. By 5:35 he'd already dawned his sweat-soaked running gear and started working on wearing out the city pavement budget. A typical 10 to 12 mile wake-up run lasted 65 minutes. Routine dictated this be followed by a ten minute shower that incorporated a religious stretching routine.

Usually the clock read 7:00 when he stepped on the scale wearing nothing but a towel. A full 90 minutes of his life had been pounded away. Multiplied by three, factor in two one-hour naps, and suddenly the daily running tally totaled close to six hours. Rod used to have a lot of friends. Now his only human contact came in the form of morning conversation with his mother. Trapped by lies about his mileage totals, he wished he had no contact at all.

It was a late August morning and sausages sizzled sweetly in the kitchen. Their seductive smell traveled down the hall and beneath the door. Rod stared at himself in the full-length mirror. He counted his ribs in order to justify the amount of food he was about to consume. He was down three pounds and up two ribs since Monday. Unable to ignore his gurgling stomach, he slapped on his shorts without underwear and rushed to the kitchen.

"Good morning love," was his mother's staple greeting. "How many links do you want?"

"Fourteen," blurted her ravenous son.

"I see you went for another run," said his mother, turning over the links. "Just an easy three, I assume."

"Yeah," replied her leery son, plucking a link from the sizzling pan.

"Stop that! You know I hate it when you grab food from the pan."

"I'm starving."

"I know! I spent $200 dollars on groceries last night. Your poor father can't get enough to eat."

"He can't?"

She shoveled several links onto a plate and gave her son a critical glare.

"I'm going to have to add cabinet space if you keep running as much as you are. Which brings up something I've been meaning to ask you ..."

Rod's cheeks puffed out to capacity.

"Why have you been lying to me about how much you've been running?"

Rod stopped mid chew. He blushed with embarrassment. Too hungry to remain in homeostasis, he resumed chewing, holding off his response until he swallowed.

"I left my log out, didn't I?"

His mother held up the sweat-stained volume. She gave him a look that only a mother can give.

"I'm not happy that you lied to me," she said.

"I'm sorry," Rod pleaded. He tried to pull another link from the pan only to get a smack on the hand.

"I don't think you should be running this much. You're going to get hurt."

"I can't afford to lose."

His mother sighed. The woman tried her best to understand. But she had never been an athlete; it was like asking an atheist to pledge allegiance to God.

"Rodney, I know you're upset about what happened last spring, but you've got to be realistic."

"I'm being realistic," he argued. "I'm doing what's necessary."

"And what if you get hurt?"

"I won't."

"Your coach doesn't think you should run this much. Don't you remember what he told you last summer?"

Rod eyed the sausage pan lustfully.

"You're too young to run so much."

"Sorry," he said. He walked to the cupboard and pulled out a box of cereal. "It has to be earned."

"Not at the expense of your health."

"What do you mean?"

He recognized his mother's serious face. Rod was overwhelmed with worry.

"One run a day."

She stated it so matter-of-factly. Rod tilted his head, not sure if he believed what he'd heard.

"What?"

"One run a day. No more three-a-days."

"You're joking."

"No," she sternly stated.

Rod poured seven servings of cornflakes into a bowl, and pondered his mother's orders.

"Pray tell, mother," he said smugly. "Working all day, just how do you intend to enforce such a rule?"

Mrs. Dillery wasn't used to such obstinate behavior. She looked evil. She let her baby have it.

"I guess I thought you would be respectful enough to obey my wishes," she seethed. "Perhaps I was wrong."

Rod regretted suggesting his plan of rebellion. Now he faced his mother's unrelenting wrath. The idea of continuing his covert running style would no longer be an option.

"Are you really planning to run while I'm gone?"

The young harrier could not lie.

"Rodney Martin! Are you really planning to run?"

The panicked runner tried defending his position. Unable to defeat the ingrained fear every child has of his mother, his arguments were full of fallacies. More irritated with every blundering attempt at disobedience, Mrs. Dillery finally shut down the running machine.

"You will run in the morning before I go to work," she ordered. "When you're done, you will hand me your running shoes, and I will take them with me."

"What?" Her idea transcended preposterous. "You can't do that!"

"I'm not letting you sacrifice your college career so that you can be assured of winning some silly high school title. You've got too much ahead of you, and as your mother, I am not going to let you throw it away on a whim. Give me your shoes."

Rod stood motionless. His breathing was double the usual volume. He tried comprehending exactly what had just happened. Suddenly, his mother took to action. She boldly strutted across the open living room. She walked straight to the entry, plucked her son's shoes off the welcome mat, and placed them in her briefcase. She left for work twenty minutes later. Fuming, Rod sat dejectedly on the couch, skipping his morning nap.

For hours, he was too upset to move. Habitually, he massaged his calves. When noon arrived, he looked anxiously out the window. He craved his fix.

"You don't have to listen to her."

He walked to his room. His sopping shorts and t-shirt were dangling from a chair. They hadn't spent an afternoon on that chair in weeks. Rod resented greatly that they would today. Off went his clothes. He swiped up the jersey and pulled it over his head. His reflection looked ridiculous in a singlet and no pants. Quickly, he pulled on the shorts.

Rod marveled at his perfectly sculpted legs in the mirror. He could almost see the blood travel to his feet as his bulging veins pulsed with each heartbeat. Covered with thick calluses, burdened with purple and black toenails, his feet were hands-down his most worthless feature. Or were they?

Rod looked out the window. Again he felt the call of his vise. Its steam rising in the summer sun, the pavement dared him to defy his orders. It beckoned him like death does the infirm. He stared down at his shredded feet. He wondered.

That night, when Mrs. Dillery returned home, a most curious thing greeted her. Red footprints trailed across the white living room carpet. They looked like animal tracks in the snow. She anxiously followed the path to her only son's bedroom. She rapped on the door. No response, so she cautiously peeked inside.

The sight of her son soundly sleeping melted her heart. He snored lightly. Gentle breaths reminded her of when he was a baby. But what was on his feet? She stepped further in.

"You didn't," she gasped under her breath.

Stained in blood, wrapped crudely around his feet, she saw her best white dishtowels. They were now a homemade bandage. Despite her pleas, her son had defied her. In the process he'd ruined her carpet and her towels. She shut the door and went to beg her husband to intervene. Once a runner himself, he refused.

"The boy's going to run. Let him. If he gets hurt then he'll stop."

"He's running a hundred fifty miles a week, Tom!"

"Well you're going to have to chain his legs together to stop him cause you've tried everything else. Christ, Louise! Let him run. There's worse things he could be doing!"

She would let him run. But there was no way she was going to like it.

Chapter VIII

The lonely summer on the trails transformed Rod into a consummate introvert. Rudely interrupting his vacation, the school year forced his reintegration into civilization. Practice felt stifling among the hordes of lesser harriers. Perturbed by their lethargic training pace, Rod longed for the sweltering, lonely days of mid-July.

Currently his thoughts were mired in different race strategies. The ride to the season's first meet was an hour old, but he hadn't said a word. Teammates shied away from sitting by their former friend. Intense to a fault, Rod had acquired a nasty demeanor over the summer. Traumatized from seeing the Cuban die on the track, he'd buried himself in his running.

Friendless, he now reaped the benefits of being more callous than the thick skin coating his toes and feet. Runners in the States have too many social distractions. But by shutting himself off from the world, Rod became like a Kenyan. With nothing to focus on but his running, he'd reached a state of training nirvana few U.S. athletes ever achieve. Achievement came with a price.

He'd infuriated his mother with his defiance. It'd

helped that he'd replaced the carpet, but from that fateful barefoot run on, his mother made it known that she was very upset. She'd no longer listen to running frustrations. Inside, this made Rod nervous.

There was no one else to talk to. Coach Rollins was a fantastic training tactician, but he had no interest in building back up a runner's crumbling confidence. If Rod suffered a mental meltdown, it could spell disaster.

His confidence had no logical reason to waiver. Not only had he logged an insane amount of mileage, but they were quality miles too. Nearly all of his miles were run below 6:30 pace and he'd even spent a fair amount of time sub-five. His body's ability to deliver oxygen virtually double what it was the previous summer, there was no sensible reason to believe he wouldn't crush the State Meet field like trash in the back of a garbage truck. But one thing wouldn't stop nagging him, the unknown rival on the trails.

Where had this training monster come from? Osseo had had a decent miler the year before, but no one capable of the blistering pace this runner had so routinely demonstrated.

Several times during the summer, he'd noticed the orange-clad harrier a great distance ahead on the trail. Not once was he able to catch him. It didn't matter that he was never within a half a mile when he started. It didn't matter that the runner was never ahead for more than a few minutes before he turned a different route. All that mattered, was that he didn't dominate the man like all the other sloths he'd encountered.

Today's meet wouldn't pit him against his foe. His

team wouldn't meet the Orioles until mid-season at the monstrous Princeton Invitational. Nevertheless, a statement needed to be made. Two top-ten finishers from the previous season would be competing at this meet, and all the media hyped this as the race to watch this weekend.

Unconditionally prepared, Rod had no fear of losing. So long as his tibia didn't shatter in a hole, the question of victory was not in doubt. What was uncertain was by how much. Aware his rival would scan the papers for the winner of this meet, he knew the importance of establishing himself as the undisputed favorite. Should he destroy the field by a wide enough margin, he knew the fear his enemy would feel. He understood the doubts that would creep into his rival's mind, festering, nagging doubts, more numerous than maggots on a corpse.

As he stepped off the bus, these doubts forged a nest in his mind too. Walking toward the course, he wondered if it were really possible to run 3.1 miles in under 14:50. While he waited for the girl's team to lay out the tarp, he felt queasy butterflies invade his stomach. After dropping his bag, he shed his sweats, tightened his shoelaces, and prepared to jog the course. He foraged out alone. As he ran along he noticed something interesting. He was the only one running. His confidence grew.

Jogging lightly, Rod negotiated the first hill of the course. He visualized how the soft grassy slope would appear with several other runners and decided that he would take the first 1,000 meters easy. If everyone went out at the speed he expected, it wouldn't be hard to put in a surge and end things quickly.

He hit the first kilometer mark on the backside of

the hill. An instinctual glance at his watch. Focus forward. Normally he would have continued on without a thought, but the delayed time that registered in his brain, forced him to look again.

Was it right? Despite giving minimal effort, the time on the watch was phenomenal. He became cognizant of the other people on the course. Strangely, it seemed they all stared in his direction. Was it an illusion, or were they really gawking as he ran? It became apparent it was not his imagination.

Marveling at the assortment of bedazzled gazes as he rumbled by, he couldn't understand why he drew such keen interest. Unaware of how he had transformed, he forgotten that most high school runners can't run 3:20 for a kilometer, let alone on their warm-up jog.

Confidence swelling, he upped his tempo as he entered the first loop through the woods. This is where he'd make his move. This would be the spot where he would devastate their hearts. Fire burning in his eyes, exhilaration rippling through his spine, he readied himself for victory.

Warm-up complete, Rod returned to the tarp and took out a book. He tuned out for a long morning wait. The meet was to be run in a non-traditional format. Rather than standard JV followed by the varsity, there would be a race for each of the top seven men. Since the races ran from slowest to fastest, Rod had nearly three hours before it was time to start his pre-race warm-up.

Ever since the Cuban incident, he had developed more the mindset of a third world dictator than a democratic hero. His concept of team was destroyed by individual ambition. As a result, he isolated himself from those he thought might hurt his performance. As his less gifted teammates suffered through inferior races, he read alone.

Finally, a quarter to twelve arrived. Rod closed his book, shrugged loose his shoulders and readied himself to run. Scalding like the spray of a poorly tuned shower, the sun's rays nearly set the grass afire. Rod was unfazed. He fondly remembered grueling workouts through such heat.

He fantasized about the ease with which he could run through such conditions and how it would cripple his opponents. They would be distracted by the heat, too focused on their misery, rather than the task at hand. He however, would abuse his body.

Rod breezed through the warm-up jog and found a solitary spot for a stretch. The heat made him as loose as a brothel, and his muscles lengthened easily. Touching his forehead to the knees, Rod basked in a comfortable pain.

His legs felt wonderful. In anticipation of the meet, he'd cut back to six miles the day before, and it resulted in semi-rejuvenation. His legs hadn't felt this much pop in months. He knew no one could touch him now.

He glanced down at his watch. Only 20 minutes remained. He dashed back to the woods to avoid the long lines of the outhouses and hung onto a tree for dear life.

"Ahhhhhhhhhhh," he moaned in ecstasy, pulling some leaves from the ground. "Ooooohhhhhhhh." The warm-up ritual was complete.

He emerged from the trees and did a stride-out to the tarp. His war-torn spikes felt lighter than socks. Calves rippling like cool waters, he jettisoned from the camp toward the start line. A lump filled the throats of every other man in uniform.

Rod took his spot in box six. His pulsing quads were the envy of every surrounding runner. One glance and they knew they had not trained as he had. Establishing a pecking order in their mind, 95% of the athletes were beaten before the sound of the gun.

Striding out again, Rod wheeled his legs like a cartoon roadrunner. Other runners tried to emulate their God by matching his distance. What they did not realize was that most of his distance was spent slowing down.

The three-minute call. Dillery jogged to the tape. Petrified faces dotted the landscape. Burdened with expectations, the number one runner of each team strode, jumped, hopped, and stretched at the line. A sizable crowd gathered, eagerly anticipating a battle. They knew not the juggernaut named Rod Dillery. Soon they would.

His last stride complete, Dillery jogged back to his place. He prepared to suffer.

"One minute," called the official. Silence enveloped the air.

Dread materialized. It crept from mind to mind and skulked in the shadows of every competitor present. As they shifted nervous legs, each soul contemplated the suffering it would endure in the coming minutes. Though utterly prepared, this suffering would afflict Rod too.

Breathing deeply, he closed his eyes. Soothing and complete, relaxation quivered down his body. The low murmur of the crowd reminded him of the constant drone of the school bus engine. Trapped within the darkness of his head, he contemplated his unenviable choices.

Within the last minute there are only two. No longer is it possible to fake an injury. No longer is it possible to claim being lost. On the line, sweats off, spikes on, only two things can be done. You either run at the blast of the gun, or you stand still, gutless and a coward.

"Ten-Seconds!"

Dillery leaned forward quaking with adrenaline. The hairs on his body bristled. Ahead lay his kingdom. It was time for to claim his rightful spot as king!

Smoke rose!

Rod Dillery exploded. His stride was smooth, and remarkably efficient. Four hundred meters in, he secured his slot behind the big guns. As he eased up to match their tempo, a relived smile spread across his jiggling face. The tempo was slower than his typical training run. He would win. Swelling with confidence, Rod upped his go point to the 800-meter mark. He would charge from the bottom of the hill.

Accustomed to the stinging rise of Limestone Hill, the small grassy knoll ahead caused Rod no duress. Trained exclusively on the marshland flats and dusty corn roads, his opponents shuddered. As the elevation began to rise Rod's boosters ignited.

A feeling of elation. Rod buried his foes in the dust of his wake. Legs churning uncontrollably, he made quick work of disposing his enemies. A tight pack of ten dwindled to two. The lone, courageous follower doomed himself to two miles of purgatory.

Rod realized he'd neglected one possibility during his earlier visualization sessions. He had ignored the possibility of being alone. Straining his ears, he listened for the sounds of trailing harriers. Fading quickly, the gurgling breath of his vanquished opponent went from sounding like a river to that of a gentle stream.

The bottom of the steep decline greeted the runners with a razor-sharp turn. Accelerating around the red flag, Rod used the opportunity to assess the situation. What he saw both delighted and disappointed him.

The brave soul, who had followed him, now festered within his oxygen depleted muscles. About thirty meters behind, a group of more intelligent runners took solace in the rapidly closing gap between themselves and second place. Gathering momentum, they prepared to make a charge. Eighty meters behind the leader, they'd already conceded victory.

Assured of his place on the podium, Rod turned his focus to the more demanding challenge of running his desired time. A sub-fifteen five kilometers requires three consecutive 4:48 miles. As the first mile mark approached, his gut told him he was not on pace.

"Four fifty-three," screamed the coach manning the painted line. The budding star knew it was time.

Rod attacked the woods. He pounded until muscles unleashed a familiar burn. At such a vicious clip, how well would he maintain? Mile after mile he'd endured the burn in practice, but such sessions were of a different intensity. Runners have searched valiantly for a perfect race simulation, but it remains elusive.

Fiery acid ravaged his legs. The lungs and heart increased productivity to meet the escalating demand. Due to their training, they adjusted. Accustomed to torment, Rod's body attained a point of survivable homeostasis.

His delicate ankles rolled precariously close to sprain amidst the uneven contours of the trail. Terrified spectators gawked when the senior rushed past. A streak of forest green, Rod appeared as an apparition, a ghost; there one moment and then gone like a sniper.

Low whispers traveled through the crowd at the edge of the forest. There were rumors of a college runner leading the race. They gathered where the runners exited the woods and waited. They waited to read the school name, screen-printed across the front. Fascinated by such dominance, they jammed around the two-mile point, anxious to hear the time. Charging from the darkness, Rod emerged from the woods. Pain combusted within his pupils and tears steamed from his ducts.

"Nine forty-three," bellowed a haggard official, an ancient relic of seasons past.

"Damn it!"

Rod forged ahead with newfound urgency. Sub-fifteen required three sub-4:48's. He'd not run one. He punished himself for his lethargy and detonated into a burst of speed straight from the depths of hell.

The cells of the brain started suffocating. His respiratory system tapped into emergency reserves, trying desperately to quell the crisis. Spots flashed across his eye. Every breath felt like it was through a straw.

"Maintain!"

The faltering harrier raged past the two and a half mile mark. Combating this self-inflicted vertigo, Rod tried in earnest to focus. But his thoughts were formless and unpredictable. His tongue slathered drool across his chin. His eyes rolled back toward his cerebellum. Impeccably trained, his muscles carried forward, instinctually following the sound of the lead golf cart.

At last he flailed around the final turn.

"One more try!" he cried.

Rod charged home. Riding the roar of the crowd, he staggered towered the finishing banner. His body was exhausted. He slowed. Ahead by over a minute, no one in the field was there to take advantage.

The last 100 felt longer than the first three miles. An optical illusion, the finish moved away with each step. A side cramp sliced at his heart. Would it ever end? Rod barely noticed when a most merciful finish line gobbled him up. He fell to the ground, hitting the dirt with a thud.

"Move along! Move along!"

Chewing on grass, clawing forward, Rod glared at the official barking instructions.

"Move along, I said!"

Why is it that track officials just don't understand? What happens over time that causes officials to forget the pain they once endured and allows them to torture young runners by forcing them forward in their moment of suffering? The words sounded jumbled inside Rod's head. Then, a heavy hand yanked him upward.

"What the ...?"

The fallen runner feebly thrashed his arms. It was a lame attempt to escape the grasp of his captor. Too exhausted to fight, he quickly relented, allowing the official to scuff his knees along the earth of the chute.

"Next time move, or I'll DQ ya," yelled the official, dropping Rod to the ground. Left for dead, the fallen victor stared at the sky. The fluids of his inner ear sloshed around his cranium. All was well with the world. Just now the other competitors started filtering in. The victory was complete and in a most staggering time of 15:01. All was well but for one thing; a biting pain ripped at the top of his leg.

Chapter IX

Dubbed the world's largest cross-country invitational, the Princeton Invite boasted over 90 teams from every corner of Minnesota. Not only was there quantity, but there was quality too. In the large school division, seven of the state's top ten ranked teams would be competing; four of the top five. Only the third-ranked Lions of Fairmont would be absent this year.

More intriguing would be the individual showcase. Nine of the top ten returning State Cross Country Meet finishers would battle for the title of the season's most important invitational. A title at the Princeton means instant credibility, instantaneous crowning as the favorite to win the ultimate prize, the State Championship.

Of particular interest would be what the media dubbed, "The Battle." Absolutely dominant in every race they'd touched, the top runner for both Park Center and Osseo had drawn extra attention to this year's meet. Both runners had won every contest they'd run, by at least 30 seconds. Today, the streak would end.

Trotting along through a vapory mist, Jeremy Sylas led our pack on a course run-through. The team had gelled in recent weeks. Three team titles and a second place ranking in the State went a long way toward preventing any internal strife. Sylas took it upon himself to be the leader and now coached us as we warmed along the grassy trail.

"Hit the turns with authority," he said at every flag. "Everybody slows on the turns. It's your chance to gain a few seconds."

Normally such advise wouldn't have sat well. But even the proud Creighton had grown to respect our new leader. Unconditionally dedicated, he'd trained with unmatched passion. Totally unselfish, he'd sacrificed two meets to lay back and push teammates along to personal bests. Militantly competitive, he'd dominated the field each time coach unlocked the shackles.

My own rise to prominence, along with his sheer dominance, elevated our team to new heights. Only top-ranked Wayzata had beaten us. Only by a slim seven points. Nearly 40-deep, our roster provided ample depth for us to be considered a State Championship contender. Today would provide the test. Sylas would test his mettle in an individual battle against the Park Center stud. The rest of us would fight in the trenches against Wayzata. Every point would count. Sylas felt the pressure. You could see it in his eyes.

Awed by the magnitude of the event, our faces were strained with stress as we dropped our sweats in box 34. The field ahead was swarming with the bodies of runners. Striding, stretching, screaming, praying, worrying, and visualizing, they milled around in their individual worlds. Five minutes later, they leaned forward as a unified line.

At the sound of the cannon, the scene looked like a medieval battlefield. Thundering forward, athletes battered the ground to submission. Trembling beneath the tonnage, the ground shook like a small earthquake. A rabid crowd added the element of a stadium cheer.

Elbows flailing, spikes spearing for tendons, I aggressively fought for position. I fixed my eyes on the horizon. My heart leapt for joy when I spotted him. A distant orange speck, Sylas was alone. Perhaps the Park Center athlete hadn't faced a runner of this caliber? Perhaps the battle all the papers so coolly predicted, wouldn't materialize at all?

Morale boosted, I doubled my efforts. If Sylas earned one point, our team had a decided advantage over Wayzata in a meet this size. Lacking a true front-runner, they would be lucky to be within ten points after one man. Were I able to finish right after him, then they'd be down ten points or more after two.

For three miles, I tore deep into the flesh of my heart. My chest collapsed inward. Tense arms locked in an immovable position. The cell count in my brain dropped dangerously low, as my body made sacrifices for the good of my core.

Every few minutes, I'd drift into a dream world. Consumed by my agony, I tried escaping within a high of endorphins. Burned to submission, my supply of the drug was inadequate. My only solace was the distant sight of Sylas running away from the field. I envied him for many reasons. For his speed and ability. For his iron will. But mostly for the fact he'd finish two minutes before me.

At around 16 minutes, I careened around the final

curve. Trapped between forest on my left and four runners on my right, my position was poor.

The blue of Wayzata's number-one was 15-meters ahead. Utterly determined, I tortured myself intolerably to try and reel him in. After I cut the gap to six or seven meters, hope raised goose bumps all across my saturated skin. My body hit the red line, but the gap wouldn't close anymore!

Hope farted away like a deflating balloon. I let out a moan and reverted to panic mode. Fifty meters remained and every point counted, but my unprepared mind played Judas!

My legs twisted into knotted cramps and my arms locked up like angle measures. My pace dissipated to a crawl. Sweat sprayed from my white, frizzy fro and salted another opponent passing me by. My face was a portrait of suffering. The tense muscles in my jaw locked my lower teeth outward like those of an Ojibwa. By the time I fell across the line, two more enemies had passed me. An official handed me my 11th place card.

As I exited the chute, an elated Sylas embraced me.

"Great run," he screamed, slapping my back. "Great run!"

Drooling on his shoulder, I didn't respond. I looked toward the finish. Creighton just finished the race of his life. The way he pumped his fist, you would have thought that he had won. Judging by how fresh he looked going through the finishing chute, I wondered why he'd not run harder.

"Holy cow, Sylas," he pronounced, joining our

team-wide hug. "You put a number on that Park Center guy! He was never in the race!"

"Quite literally," our star coolly responded.

"What'ya mean?"

"He wasn't in the race."

Creighton gave Sylas a look of bewilderment. Through my stupefied gaze, I managed to convey a sense of confusion as well.

"There's no way a sub-fifteen guy was in that race. He must be injured or something."

Creighton looked at the ground.

"What a coward," he said. "He probably faked an injury so he wouldn't have to face you."

Rolling his eyes, Sylas gave his rival more credit than even he thought he deserved.

"C'mon, Creighton. There's a million reasons he might not have run. Don't cut him down if you don't know."

"Bull!" declared Creighton ambivalently. "That guy's a coward!"

I was too tired to join the conversation.

Sylas changed the subject.

"How'd Markson and Busch do?" he asked. Glancing at the chute, we could see our four/five coming up the line. Nearer the front than the rear, things looked encouraging. Sylas rushed to greet them, his ulterior motive to grab the place cards and do some calculations. He ripped the cards from their hands. For several moments he stared down at the orange papers, frantically tallying in his head. Creighton was better at arithmetic and jumped first.

"Sixty-four points," he screamed, charging in my

direction. "We got it! Ha haaaaaaaa! We got it!"

Too drained to move, I happily accepted his tackle by falling to the ground. Soon I was mobbed from all directions, a gravitational senior centerpiece for celebration.

Despite my fatigue, it felt wonderful. It was a feeling of collective pride like none I've ever experienced before or since. My spine tingled with excitement. I could only dream of the feeling one would get at the moment they knew they'd won a State Cross Country Meet. I would have gone on fantasizing forever, but I saw something that struck me as odd.

Through the numerous limbs piled atop me, I saw Jeremy Sylas sitting off to the side. It shocked me that he wouldn't join in the melee. Then it hit me. In spite of the team triumph, his day was incomplete. The absence of the Park Center runner left a gaping hole in his resume.

Longingly, he gazed across the course, wondering about the confrontation that hadn't happened. You could see the spirit of competition begging to escape. It would be condemned to prison for at least another three weeks. Would it be shackled forever? We wouldn't know until the next confrontation, the State Meet.

Chapter X

Dimly lit, the doctor's waiting room felt cold and forbidding. Rod slouched back dejectedly in his chair. He examined the room without thought. Magazines flowed out from a rack on the wall. Posters covered every inch of the dingy tan wallpaper. Rod's upper right leg writhed in pain.

Four meets into the season, he'd never won by less than 45 seconds. At the last meet he'd broken fifteen. But with each dominating performance, the leg hurt more, deteriorating like the old central city. Every fifteen-mile day increased the pain. At first only after runs, but then it evolved into more. Constantly pulsing and throbbing, it was his entire existence.

He'd iced, stretched, visualized and medicated; nothing worked. Fearful that his leg might crack, he approached his mother and asked to go to the doctor.

"Don't talk to me about your running problems," she said callously. "You made your choice."

Lowering his head, Rod knew he'd have to compromise. Knowing full well his mother wouldn't pull any punches, he made an offer he thought she couldn't refuse.

"I'll go to one run a day, no Princeton Invite."

"How can I trust you to run once a day?"

Rod paused.

"Because, I don't have a choice."

"You'll have to do better than that," she said angrily. "Don't have a choice. Sounds like you'd be doing one run a day whether you see the doctor or not."

Point taken, Rod sat stewing in silence. "I'll take a week off and the Princeton Invite."

"And if that Doctor says don't run, you don't run." Rod grimaced. She was cruel.

"Okay," he agreed reluctantly.

In spite of her anger, Rod's mother kept her end of the bargain. The next day he sat in the waiting room. With the Princeton the following day, he clung to slim hope that perhaps the injury would prove inconsequential. Hope is an opiate for those who don't have any.

A light rap cracked on the door. Rod smiled, seeing the familiar face of the family physician Dr. Bryce. Irritatingly cheery, he greeted Rod with a handshake.

"Hey Rod! How are things going?"

"Fine."

"How's your mom?"

"Fine."

"And how are things going with you?"

"I've got a pain in my leg."

"Running ... I assume?"

"It started that way." Rod paused. "Now it hurts all the time."

"Upper leg, lower leg?"

Rod touched the top of his thigh. He stared at the spot while explaining.

"Right across the top here. It throbs all the time, especially when I hit the ground with my stride."

Dr. Bryce took hold of Rod's ankle. The good doctor started twisting and tweaking in all directions. Knee to the chest, turned to both sides, no particular movement seemed to aggravate the area more than another. When he was finished, Dr. Bryce frowned and sat back on his stool pondering the possibilities.

"Is it deep, or more toward the surface," he queried.

"Deep. It feels like the bone."

"And you say it hurts mostly when your stride hits the ground?"

"It started that way. Now it just hurts all the time though."

Rod anxiously awaited diagnosis. He glared at the doctor with a look of concern. The doctor sighed.

"There's several possibilities," he started. "It could be a strain of the deep muscle tissue; in which case we could try an anti-inflammatory and ice."

"I've been taking so many anti-inflammatories that my stomach is probably mush," interjected the soft-spoken harrier.

"Have ..."

"Ice too ... religiously."

Dr. Bryce pinched the bridge of his nose between two fingers. Hesitantly, he moved to possibility number two.

"Well there's also the possibility of stress fracture.

Have you been running more miles than usual?"

Nodding sadly, Rod affirmed the doctor's worst fears.

"Your symptoms add up to a stress fracture of the femur," he said somberly. "I'd recommend doing an x-ray and going from there."

Half an hour later, Doctor Bryce pulled Rod out to the hall and placed two x-rays on the light board. After studying them for a second, he proceeded to launch into an explanation. He pointed to a dark glitch on the side-shot.

"That, right there, appears to be a crack," he said firmly.

He paused a moment, craning his face closer for a better look.

"Definitely a crack." He turned toward Rod and gave his long-time patient even more bad news.

"And when the crack shows up on x-ray, it usually means it's a darn pretty good one."

Rod walked back to the exam room and sat down in a stunned, cold, silence. Dr. Bryce followed, closing the door softly behind. Despite Rod's glazed expression, he started talking treatment options. They were few and unattractive.

"Really the only thing you can do to cure a stress fracture is rest," he explained. Rod rolled his eyes upward. He wanted to cry. "In the case of a crack this big, you might be talking six to eight weeks."

"What happens if I run?"

A deep exhale.

"It might crack and damage the hip joint." He paused.

"And that, well that would be a disaster."

Rod bit down on his lip 'till it bled. Trickling across his tongue, the blood tasted like the iron-heavy water of a park fountain. Only the burden on his heart felt heavier. Holding back the tears, he desperately searched for a glimmer of hope.

"If I cut back my mileage, can it hold up for three weeks?"

"It's tough to say," the Dr. said hesitantly. "It really depends on the person."

"What do you mean by disaster?"

"I mean you'd probably never run again. You may even have trouble walking normally."

Rod felt like cold-cocking the doctor. He knew it wasn't his fault, but he didn't care. He wanted to run. He needed to run. Too much was invested to stop.

"If I run, I'll win State."

Rod's confidence caught the doctor by surprise. A former runner himself, he appreciated Rod's dilemma. The ultimate question arose.

"Do you want to run in college?" he asked.

Rod cried. He knew exactly where the doctor was going. It was a catch 22. On one hand, Rod couldn't imagine the possibility of a career-ending injury. On the other, he was unable to fathom the agony of falling short of his goal.

The rain spattering across the windshield on the ride home was reflective of Rod's mood. Though the diagnosis hadn't shocked him, the reality of it had. Only one thing would be more difficult than making the choice he was faced with: lying to his mother again.

She'd been waiting patiently on the living room sofa for his return, and the moment he arrived the interrogation started. Ten minutes in, he wondered when she'd put him on the rack.

"Just a strain," she voiced suspiciously. "Just a strain. I think I'll give Dr. Bryce a call."

Rod found it difficult to hide the movement of his Adam's apple. Stress made him swallow. The saliva nearly drowned him.

"I'm not saying he didn't recommend I rest," he pleaded, as she walked toward the phone. "He did. But he also said it could wait 'till after State."

Technically he was telling the truth. For some strange reason, the subconscious hint of truthfulness in his voice caused his mother to refrain from calling.

"Fine," she conceded. "I won't call. But if I see one hint of a problem the next time you run, then we're going back to the doctor, and I'm going with you!"

His world crumbling around him, Rod stood defeated. Teammates alienated, parents infuriated, body decimated, he had little left. Quietly he tiptoed to his room. Lying down on his bed, Rod stared blankly at the ceiling. It was then that he had a revelation. It was then that he made his choice.

"Better to risk and fail than to never risk at all," he whispered. Exhausted, he dozed off to sleep, dreaming all the while of his State Meet run.

Chapter XI

Jeremy Sylas locked the door and drew the shades of his bedroom. Though the furnace valiantly fought the cool front that swept in that afternoon, it did nothing to take away the nervous chills he was feeling. The Class AA Cross Country Final was less than 24 hours away. An innocent looking section of the newspaper lay open on the bed. It was there that Sylas learned his rival had qualified for State in 14:49.

Several times, his mother came to the door because he had a phone call. No doubt friends were calling to arrange the traditional pre-State dinner. Sylas pretended to sleep. He just couldn't bear the thought of going out. He wanted time. If he went out and passed away the evening with his friends, then the race would arrive sooner. Secretly he hoped that if he stayed within the confines of his room, that time might stop, and he could spend eternity knowing the pain would never come.

He knelt down by his bed and prayed. God probably didn't care, but prayer always brought him comfort. It was a greedy prayer, a prayer full of requests.

"Please let me have a good race. Please take away

the nerves. I know this is my gift. Let me give it back tomorrow."

Sylas laid his head down on the bed. He focused on his breathing and prayed harder. But the harder he prayed the more nervous he got. God wasn't listening. And so he stopped. How long he stopped, he didn't know. What he did know, is that when he woke up on the bedside floor, the sun had set and the clock had advanced three hours.

A rap on the door.

"It's time for dinner, Jeremy."

He rubbed his eyes.

"Did you hear me sweetie?"

Even his mother's voice seemed chilling.

"Yeah, mom. I'll be there in a minute."

A minute turned to two, then three, then nine. Sylas never left the floor. He sat with his legs spread wide, trying to get a stretch in. The lock popped on the door. Jeremy's father lumbered in.

"Dinner's on the table, son," he sternly said. "We're waiting to say grace."

Sylas knew he'd need all the grace that God could muster. He extended his hand and let his father pick him up. Now the question was would God pick him up tomorrow?

Chapter XII

A fierce gale cracked against Rod's bedroom window. Branches from the backyard birch tree scratched up against the glass. It sounded like a gremlin trying to get inside. Huddled beneath warm flannel sheets and a thick down comforter, Rod was a shivering insomniac.

The moonlight reflected brightly off the clock. It read 2:10. Rod watched the minute hand slowly crawl from the one to the two. The consistency of the change was irritating. It reminded him of summer. It reminded him of how consistently he'd logged mile after mile.

Biting like a viper, the pain in his leg returned with a vengeance. It kept him from his precious sleep. Each time he closed his eyes, it struck. It came from his thigh, stabbing from the inside out.

Disgustedly, Rod tossed off the covers. His bladder wasn't full, but nervous irritation fooled the nerves of his urethra. Standing before the porcelain basin, he stared blankly at the portrait of a Spanish water girl. It was the third time he'd seen her that night.

He hurried back to his room, crawled into bed and pulled the covers to his chin. Each time an icy snowflake pelted up against the window, he dreaded more how cold he'd feel that morning. There'd be no wrap of blankets on the course. Naked, but for a pair of short shorts and a skimpy singlet, every breath of wind would bite through his pale, white skin.

Perhaps he wouldn't run. He had an out. It was legitimate. Instead of suffering, he could stand off on the sidelines. He knew that if he were in the race, it wouldn't be close. With six weeks rest, he could heal his shattered femur and still have three months practice before the start of track. If his leg held up, he'd win the mile. It wouldn't be a contest.

Naturally, reality counter-attacked. Cross-country is every distance runner's true love. Track is just a late-spring mistress. That summer, Rod had saturated the earth with a flood of sweat and tears, shedding blood when his shoes were taken hostage. He had more invested in this race than a lifetime investor in the market. To sit was not an option. Victory could only be achieved by taking risks.

Sinking further beneath his sea of covers, Rod tried hiding from the world. Enshrouded by the darkness, he relaxed, not having to watch the ceaseless changing of the clock. Time was the enemy. Time always ticked away too fast.

Right now it was the cushion between tranquility and suffering. But the hours ticked away like minutes, and the minutes disappeared like seconds. At 10:00 that morning, the apparent flow of time would reverse itself abruptly. Though the minutes would continue passing at their rhythmic pace, no longer would they feel quick and easy.

Immersed in pain, Rod would grapple with his human limitations, conscious of each thousandth of a second. When you view those thousandths on a stopwatch they fly by with untraceable rapidity. When you're driving forward screaming legs, lungs contracting upon your heart, you can feel each fraction of a second etch itself upon your soul.

When you're suffering, you simply long to curl up amidst the waving grasses along the trailside. Beckoned by primitive recollections of the womb, your one desire is to return to where there is no pain.

In Minnesota, thousands flock to see this agony the first weekend of each November. Unable to understand why young boys engage in such suicidal endeavors, they pay their measly entry fee and line normally empty wooded trails. For 20 minutes they witness suffering not seen outside of war and famine. Rod dreaded such suffering. Yet he craved it too.

Shrouded by his linen casket, Rod hoped the night would continue on forever. Only Einstein's theories could save him now. Unable to comprehend or even fathom using his list of excuses, he begged God for a stoppage of the clock.

However, as has been said before, divinity keeps its hands off of distance running. It is a strictly human undertaking of which God will play no part. A runner in his race has no recourse but to die.

The awful buzzing of his alarm startled Rod awake. He stared unwaveringly at the digits before him. His mind was in a state of utter disbelief. The clock said 6:00. In four short hours the trial would begin.

Chapter XIV

Rod descended the steps of the bus and planted his feet on the earth. He took a moment to soak up the atmosphere. Several in the blocked line behind him, grumbled. Commanding victories built celebrity and a large entourage had hopped on the bandwagon. Expecting sure victory, even non-running fans had latched on for the trip.

Rod cared nothing about the group. As if to spite them, he took his time scanning the landscape. State Meets never got old. They were like fine chocolate candy, sweet to the last savory bite. A senior now, he held the last square in his mouth. Sentiment grabbed him firmly. Breathing deeply, he sadly closed his eyes. He felt like a dying man watching the sunset. He was awed by its magnificence, but silently prayed for time.

The note of a French horn rang out. A familiar running classic, the Chariots of Fire melody began. Rod dropped his bags and jogged straight for the start line, inspiration egging him on. Enamored with their hero, others would carry his bags the rest of the way to the field house.

As the music cried out, his body responded. Bubbling up from his skin, goose bumps covered him. Standing attention, the hairs of his body paid homage to the song. Adrenaline flowed freely. His jog became a run. His run became a stride.

Everyone recognized him. He was the favorite. All others parted out of the way. A god in these circles, they dare not block his line. Some hollered, some cheered, some gawked, a few jeered, but none dared to approach the almighty. By the time Rod arrived at box six, he appeared a like a lion in the open savannah. From a distance, his prey watched with a sense of foreboding.

Rod gazed across the grassy tundra. He closed out the world. Focus drawn inward, all doubt was erased. He'd memorized the course in prior competition and now ran it in his mind. Fourteen-minutes and twenty-nine seconds later, he stopped. "Live like a clock," he had heard. Such a slave he was, even his visualizing was done in perfect time.

When he got back to the field house, reporters were already lurking. Coach Rollins fought honorably, but the numbers were too great for him to protect his prodigy. A lesser mind might have crumbled. Rod expected it. There was nothing to stop him this time. Not even the death of the second place runner.

As flash bulbs popped, Rod stretched in silence. He contentedly listened to the drone of humanity. On the rare occasion he glanced up from his meditation, there was an immediate flurry of media questions. He always looked back down without answer. This caused the reporters much agitation. Consumed with his task, he would not succumb to the trap of becoming celebrity. No championships to his credit, he didn't deserve the attention, even if he had been dubbed "Gentleman Rod," the runner who'd sacrificed winning to help a competitor.

At 9:15 Rod rose from his stretching and trotted outside for his warm-up. It was the one time the reporters did not follow. They were too burdened by their cameras, pencils, pens, and rolls of fat. For twenty minutes Rod reveled in the peace of the woods. Then he returned to his spot to stretch again. Creatures of habit, the reporters kept hunting. Anyone stubborn enough to run 170 miles a week is stubborn enough to ignore media pressure. Rod remained silent.

Up to this point, Coach Rollins had left his prize runner alone. All season he'd kept his hands off. Even when mom called, concerned about the training log, he never betrayed his pupil. Instead, he opted to let fate determine his destiny. When coach squatted down next to Rod, it surprised his runner. Indebted to his mentor for his support, Rod took time to listen carefully. Painfully curious, the crowd hushed up to listen too.

"There's no one more prepared," whispered coach.

"It's time."

Brevity was beauty. Rod looked at the clock. Ten minutes to ten, the moment had come. It was time to go claim his prize. A media circus accompanied him to the line. His focus was strong, hands down the strongest, but for one rare exception.

When he arrived at the line, another throng of reporters was already there. Circled round the Osseo camp, they came for one reason, to follow his rival in orange. The two titans crossed paths as he jogged to his box. Their eyes met. For a moment, focus was swallowed by emotion. For the first time all season, they'd meet, two superpowers, battling it out amidst the also-rans. Feeling the chill of his nerves, Rod tried hard to refocus his thoughts.

"Too many miles. You ran too many miles to lose."

As he shed his sweats, he said it over and over. Biting his lip, he tried hard to believe. Fear is the companion of runners. Even the elite can't escape its dark shadow. Trembling as he started his strides, even Rod fell victim. Even now, before the race, he swore he heard footsteps behind.

But when he turned, the orange clad devil was nowhere in sight. Still back at the line, he'd not moved. Instead, he waited for his own moment to shine.

As Rod moved back toward the line the devil started. Sculpted by God, mighty muscles bulged every inch from waist down. Uncommonly quick, the pace was sheer horror. Rod doubted.

"I can't be that fast."

And for several more minutes the round-robin stride-show continued. Each time, the runners upped the ante when it came his time. Too confident to back down, too familiar to let it pass, the two runners sprinted into a pre-race rage. They'd have postured forever had it not been for the National Anthem.

Rod's body reached critical stage. His heart thumped. His head swam with a million thoughts. When the anthem ended, two minutes remained. Nauseous and jittery, Rod hopped, leaped, and stretched like a mad man. Then he completed his last stride out. Only worrying remained. Jangled nerves fired away uncontrollably. Sickened by butterflies, Rod's mind flooded with uncertainty. Nervousness reigned. His face cringed. Rod wanted nothing more than for it to all go away.

"Ten seconds," blared the P.A. The state's finest athletes leaned forward.

It happened to Rod each State Meet when he stepped up to the line. Having come to grips with the inevitable, the body responded peculiarly. He thought he would feel unbearable angst, but it was total relaxation instead. His limbs dangled, and he marveled at why he was ever nervous at all. His mind responded to the visualizing, and banished all doubt.

Smoke rose from the gun, followed by an ominous crack! Tearing from the line, Rod bolted straight for the front. His elbows bruised everyone who got in his way. One harrier crumpled to the ground, but no recall was ordered.

By one-quarter mile, the show had begun! Two warriors, one dressed green and one orange, clashed like two knights in full armor. Fueled by irrational hatred, they fought with vulgar intensity. Their dream match materializing, the crowd erupted with similar passion.

The enemies entered the arena of rolling hills with a sharp turn to the right. At such breakneck speed, these mogul sized mounds had a roller coaster like quality. Stomachs dropping, legs driving, each runner tested the other with small, unplanned surges. Since both were accustomed to minor discomfort, neither gained much from such trivial exchanges.

It wasn't until the two warriors careened over the last of the bumps that Rod unleashed a volley of speed not yet unshackled this race. "Gravedigger Hill" was a mile ahead. He hoped to frighten the devil with courage.

Immediate results of the charge were encouraging. Daunted by such a flurry of speed so close to the hill, the runner in orange laid back. Stoked by success, Rod shifted to another gear. He'd end it now, while his opponent reeled in his thoughts. For several moments, the sounds of the footsteps behind faded, but then ... they thundered back.

There was too much at stake to fold early. The runner in orange was ready to fight. Defying pain, he charged back up to the front. The crowd erupted.

Seething with fury, Rod looked right. He worried. The runner in orange showed no obvious signs of duress. Comfortably matching his menace each stride, the devil looked left. Their eyes met.

Staring deep into the black of his opponent's dark pupils, Rod saw something not evident when he took his first glance. There, deep within the eyes of another, he saw agony. He felt liberated. He was set free by his discovery and charged Gravedigger Hill with kamikaze-like zeal.

His rival followed, but the breathing beside Rod grew steadily more labored. Knees driving, arms pumping, Rod fought harder. As he crested the hill, he tormented his body with his iron-fast mind. His opponent kept up, but his spirit dangled by a razor-thin thread. Rod flourished listening to the wheezing.

Descending the hill nearly cost Rod his life. He disregarded all caution and let gravity rest his suffering legs. It was this childlike recklessness that severed the thread keeping his rival alive. At the hill's base, Rod looked right. Nothing! No fluttering cheeks, no pained eyes, just woods and an occasional spectator.

With the enemy broken, the task grew more dangerous. Unsure of the battles brewing behind, he recalled the warm breath across his back during that fateful mile last track season. He tightened the vise.

His diaphragm was strained. A wicked side cramp sliced at his lungs. But he didn't slow down. Prepared for such trials, he pictured the pain burning off. Slowly it moved from his side to his front. Then it dispersed through his body and nested itself in his leg. With a mile remaining his mind was intact, but the crack in his leg now loomed largely.

Once smooth and efficient, his stride developed a hitch on the left. In a panic, he looked back to check on his lead. Nobody there.

Sensing his struggles, the crowd urged their new hero on.

"You're alone! The record's in reach!"

Rod clenched his teeth and dug deeper. With each stride, his limp grew like an untreated virus. The question of "if" became "when."

Hot blood knifed at his femur. He had no concern about breathing or the acid building up his calves. Nothing left to lose, he burst into a kick with three quarters to go. Pain tore at the tendons and muscles lining his pelvis. The leader's duress caused a great stir in the crowd.

Swelling with the force of a hurricane flood, his lead reached legendary proportions. With 800 to go he had over 100 meters. Long since demoralized, the rival in orange had not thrown in the towel, but conceded the victory and pressed on for time. Rod would finish alone. Aside from the injury, only his personal demons could stop him now.

He turned the last corner.

Rod's brain smoldered from sensory overload. As he careened around the final curve, the space between each breath diminished. Subconscious songs of his creation played in his head. With each step, the volume shifted upwards. Long before he'd break the tape, the melody would become intolerable. Each note of breath manufactured agony, a mystical fire that stimulated every pain producing nerve he had. As it droned on faster and faster, each beat, tightened the vise around his chest. Every pump of the heart hurled lactic acid up his legs.

This acid ate up his bone. Made brittle by summer pounding, it only held him up by a thread. Every step caused it to crumble. Rod turned his focus to his watch and chastised his leg with a curse. He'd been running for 14:15. Sub-14:30 was in reach!

His vision turned to double and the word finish became two. As his body died, the cells of his brain started blackening. Half a track length remained. Rod summoned every neuron he had, and ordered them to fire his legs forward. The drudgery was complete. His goal of a championship touched the tips of his fingers. With each meter, the fist of his hand closed further up. It rose upward on the end of his jubilant arms. Rod felt the first chills of a championship, when suddenly he heard a deafening ...

"Crack!"

Rod crumbled. His shoulder plowed through the sod. Paralyzed by shock, he lay still; his once insurmountable lead now withering away. Pain cleaved at his mutilated hip joint, but it was nothing compared to the sting in his mind.

He weakly lifted his head. Dirt and grass fell from his face. Longingly, he stared at the line he was so sure he'd cross. Twenty meters away, it beckoned him. Driving his fingers into the sod, he began clawing. The mute crowd erupted.

Rod slithered home meter by meter. He knew his adversary was close. The steady crescendo of the partisan crowd, warned him that danger was now at a critical level. Only ten meters separated the harrier from the one thing he desired. Exerting every last scrap of his will, he shunned pain. He dragged his broken body toward home. But the body rebelled.

Consumed by shock, his claws retracted. The damaged body instinctually curled into a fetal ball. The goal unrealized, his hope now rested on the goodness of others. This time he'd earned it, but the question became, would someone less deserving take it away.

He could hear footsteps. Would his rival remember Rod's selfless deed from the previous spring? Had he the honor to aid this fallen gladiator across the line, giving him what he so richly deserved? The crowd buzzed with anticipation. The runner in orange arrived!

Barreling forward, he tore past his fallen rival and raised triumphant arms! Two factions of crowd showed their allegiances, as a mixture of loud cheers and cruel jeers erupted.

Rod never heard the noise. His head dropped to the dry, November grass, and he moistened parched earth with his tears. His hip destroyed, he would never do what he loved more than anything else ever again.

Chapter XV

For the first time in my life, the sound of the gun brought needed relief. The media fracas surrounding Sylas and his Park Center rival was out of control. We'd barely been able to escape for our warm-up, let alone prepare for our race. We never had a chance to focus on the task at hand.

For Sylas, it was a simple one. And as I watched him boldly match the Park Center runner stride for stride, I was astounded by how quickly they formed a gap between themselves and the remainder of the field. Only an ignorant fool from a far off section tried to match them. He was All-State material, but due to his idiocy, would only end up beating four other runners in the race.

Meanwhile, my own little world was growing rapidly more turbulent. Wedged tightly in a pack of ten between fifteenth and twenty-fifth in the race, I found the conditions rather rough and the personalities quite hostile. At first I was content to watch Sylas battle it out at the front of the race, but a bony elbow changed my priorities quickly.

Lashing back, I disregarded coach's lecture on

sportsmanship and left a black and blue reminder on the shorter runner's face. Several souls in heaven cringed when they heard what he called me next. Words didn't bother me. I just cut him off, farted, and let him fester in the stench. From there, I surged to the front of the small pack where I resided. I caught sight of Sylas in the distance. Currently his life was much more harrowing than to what he was accustomed.

A running machine, the runner in green yielded nothing since the opening shot. Pace steady, he pounded as mercilessly now, as he had the first 400 meters. This grueling tempo never waned in intensity. It was more than Sylas cared to handle so early. He closed his eyes. He made a choice to accept the cruelty of his fate.

It hurt. It hurt a lot. His grueling summer had laid the foundation, allowing him to suffer, but just half a mile in, every mile he'd logged was called to arms. It was now a test of mental fortitude. The body was ready, but was the mind? He had to know! And so began the early tests.

Sylas hammered ahead with a reckless surge. His intent was to send the message. He controlled the race. Both runners careened over the first of several grassy moguls at their mile-race pace. Sylas just wanted to gain a meter; something to bolster his confidence.

But the teal-clad warrior grew enraged by such a trial. Instantly responding, he drew up on Sylas' side before reaching the next mogul's base. Breathing heavily, he need not make his presence known. Sylas saw him from the corner of his eye.

The two rivals bobbed across the uneven terrain. Lined with rabid spectators, a snarled roar was sharp in contrast to the pleasant sounds of Elm Creek Park. Sylas was having trouble breathing. Despite his summer training, the vicious pace threw his system into shock. For someone who had cowered out of an earlier invite, his rival had no qualms about setting a precarious pace.

Everything about this run simply reeked of pain. His legs burned like a jet-fuel fire. Falling half a step behind his rival, Sylas took the first step of a dying runner. He checked behind to see just how hard he'd have to run to stay in second place. It just so happened that coach limped up to the trailside at the moment of that fatal glance. Glasses steaming, the old coach let Sylas have it.

"What are you looking back for," screamed the one man capable of saving him. "It's not a minefield! Run!"

Sylas was bolstered by the stinging tirade and dug deeper in his well. What came up was a half-filled bucket. Ignoring his failing systems, he miraculously returned to his earlier breakneck pace. Somehow he managed to loosen up his rigid form and forge ahead to take the lead. For several moments he was as alone. It was just like all those lonely summer runs. But as he reveled in his accomplishment, his focus slipped for just an instant, and there he was. That cruel, ugly demon, unwilling to die, he'd come to race.

Gravedigger Hill loomed in the distance and Sylas felt pangs of panic. Glancing left, he stared straight into the evil eyes of his menacing aggressor.

Expectation proved an irksome bother; Sylas saw no sign of agony in the other's eyes. As he focused back ahead, he swallowed deeply. They hurtled recklessly toward the base of his impending doom. A grassy spiral staircase, Sylas swore the hill was inching upward each time he took a stride.

Both runners blasted upward like a space shuttle. The two fierce rivals fought their first true battle of the race. Arms locking from heinous pace, Sylas prayed for mercy.

"Just let me die," he murmured, gazing longingly at the soft grass on the trailside. "Let me fall and sleep."

But God seldom answers prayers of runners in a race. Running is an individual accomplishment and divine intervention simply wouldn't be fair. And so despite its fatigue, his heart kept pounding. Unable to deliver oxygen at an adequate pace, his lungs still breathed. And although they cramped worse than airline seating, his legs continued turning.

Groans escaped his mouth and slobber foamed across his lips. His eyes were more curious than a peeping tom's. Now he constantly assessed his opponent by the expression on his face. Never cracking, eerily monotonous, it changed little with the elevation. Relaxed and fluid, it bode poorly for Sylas' chances in the race.

Despite his agony, Sylas matched his oppressor up the hill and eagerly anticipated letting nature pull him down. It was beautiful to see the top. For a moment hope returned. He would let his long and lanky stride stretch out and rest himself on the hill's downward face. Thinking the advantage his, Sylas upped the ante for a second. His rival suddenly unleashed the full fury of his power.

Sylas felt the wind, but couldn't respond to such a flurry. By the time he reached hill's bottom, his opponent had hoarded fifteen meters cushion. Sylas tasted the salt of his tears. He was defeated. He glanced back to check on his hold on second place. All he saw was the back of the hill, laughing at his cowardice.

Rapidly decelerating, he entered very dangerous territory. Isolated, he toiled in no man's land. He was defeated by the man ahead, but insurmountably ahead of all behind. With a mile to go things could get ugly in a hurry, especially after going out at such a scalding pace.

How long he lingered in limbo he never could recall, but were it not for the voice of old hobble hip, he might have lingered there forever.

"It's not done! Go get him!"

A good hundred meters back with less than half a mile to go, Sylas could have shrugged it off. But there was something in that voice, like a whip, it urged him on. Sylas became a man.

All the pain he'd endured was nothing compared to this. Priming up his engines, he revved up his exhausted motor and burst into a finishing kick. Pride still mattered, and Sylas dug deep to show his.

Up ahead, the Park Center runner turned the final corner to the finish. He had about three hundred to go with a hundred meter lead. Sylas knew he wouldn't win, but was determined to close the gap. Blistering down the run of tall evergreens, he fed off the crowd's polite encouragement.

When he turned the corner, his rival was closer, not close enough, but he'd keep fighting. Sylas closed his eyes and scrunched his face into a mess. Horrible music enveloped him. Interwoven within harsh spastic breaths, it was a melody fit for an invalid. Combined with the large wail of the crowd, it brought forth images of murder and banshees. The crowd roared. The new champion must have finished. Sylas opened his eyes to witness all he'd lost.

His eyes went wide. His rival was on the ground, staggering toward home! Sylas' spine became electric. Adrenaline levitated him an inch off the ground.

The word finish came closer and closer. Still straggling onward, the green monster closed within ten meters of the line. Sylas grit his teeth and pushed harder. Spitting curses, he pumped once dead arms with authority. And then the rival in green curled up. He conceded the title! All of Sylas' suffering wouldn't be for naught. Victory was his, and he'd take it!

Then, Coach limped into the corner of the young runner's eye. His expression was revolting, his gaze comatose. Something was wrong in the old man's world. Sylas couldn't tell what, but it gnawed at his stomach. Thirty meters remained and he was faced with an impossible choice.

Should he take what he earned, or play the gentleman's game? Would the team forgive him for stopping, perhaps giving up the title, or would they respect him for good of his deed? The line perilously close, the choice had to come now.

Running in third, I turned the corner in time to be a witness.

I nearly fainted when my immortal teammate stopped short of the line. Crouching down, he paused, and then lifted the body of his rival. The crowd roared wildly. The two bitter rivals crossed the line together. Breathless, I dropped to fifth and never recovered. When it was all said and done, I stood vomiting at the end of the chute. Sylas came up behind me and said something I didn't expect.

"I'm sorry."

I didn't understand why.

Chapter XVI

The mood was tense inside the field house. At first I'd not understood Sylas' apology, but when I relayed to Creighton what had happened, all hell broke loose within the ranks.

"He what?" His voice was calm, but I didn't like his face. "Tell me he didn't. Tell me he didn't!"

Grabbing my shoulders, Creighton tried to give me the adult version of Shaken Baby Syndrome.

"He helped the green guy across the line." Oblivious to the significance of the incident, my voice had not yet reached Creighton's decibel level.

"Did he touch him? Tell me he didn't touch him!"

I looked over at Sylas, who was changing to his warm-ups in the corner of our camp. He heard every word, but kept on dressing as if he'd been born deaf.

"It looked like it."

"We're done. We're done! He's D.Q.'d!"

"What'ya mean?"

"If you physically aid another runner you're D.Q.'d!"

This was news to me. I looked back at Sylas hoping

for an explanation. Since he was still putting on his top, I had to listen to Creighton rant some more instead.

"What was he thinking? That idiot. You hear me Sylas? You idiot!"

Creighton shook his fist in Sylas' face. He gave no thought to the valiant nature of the deed. His tirade was drawing attention away from the stage where awards would soon take place. Sylas looked up. He said nothing.

"You moron, Sylas! You wouldn't have done that if you were a senior. Did you think about us seniors? We don't get another chance you sorry son of a .... We'll never have your talent! You can ...

"What can he do," thundered coach, eyes ablaze with the fire of a thousand suns. "What was he supposed to do?"

Creighton's legs quivered beneath the quaking voice of God. He stood speechless. All around the crowd waited silently for God to speak again.

"Don't pin the blame on him! If you had a tenth the heart of Sylas, you'd have been right there with him and won the title yourself."

Limping forward, coach looked feeble, but frightening. I'd never seen the limp so large. Six inches from Creighton's face, he sneered foully and continued on.

"I used to think like you did Creighton. I thought exactly that way. I was consumed by it. So consumed, I gave up everything to win ... And it nearly killed me when I didn't."

Tears were in his eyes.

"For years I regretted what I did. All those miles. You have no idea what it's like to run those miles. If anyone should be screaming it's him. Every day he put himself on the line. Three times a day. Morning, noon, and night! In the sun, rain, heat, snow, it didn't matter. Without him you'd have never been close to a title! Don't criticize him now!"

Coach was too furious to continue. Finally, after a lengthy pause, he managed to finish what he had to say.

"There's no guarantees in running Creighton. It's an act of faith. Sometimes it breaks your heart. It broke mine ..."

A reporter who'd heard about the incident, interrupted.

"Coach! Coach, can I have a word?"

Coach turned his head and stared him down.

"My guy didn't win. I have nothing else to say."

"But don't you think the whole situation is eerily similar to your own collapse in '63?"

Coach stood speechless. His mind drifted back to that day. The day he'd earned his championship, only to have his hip give way. The day the 1,000 summer miles he'd banked became worthless. The day a lesser runner took what he'd rightfully deserved.

He could still feel the grass in his hands as he clawed toward that finish line, the dirt on his face from his fall, the cramps as his body curled into the fetal position. The pain of a lifetime knowing he didn't win ... and never would.

But then he remembered Sylas' selfless deed. He remembered his own, that day so long ago when he'd given up his title to help the fallen Cuban. A hint of a smile touched his lips. It'd taken two-thirds of his life, but he finally realized that the title he'd craved for 40 years wasn't what really mattered. What mattered was the spirit of the sport.

So with his right hip still burning, his trophy-case still empty, coach Rod Dillery limped away. He'd have to wait at least another year to win his championship, but he'd finally found his peace of mind.

Acknowledgments

The number of people who contributed to my dream of publishing this book is far too great to list, so I'll extend my apologies ahead of time to anyone I may accidentally exclude.

My first thanks goes to my wife Anna. She's been a constant source of encouragement through the whole process, as well as a critical ear.

Two mentors who have been very instrumental in my writing are Paul Salsini and Scott Heywood. Salsini is a Marquette University Professor who took me under his wing as an undergrad and helped with the first edit of this book. Heywood was a high school English teacher whose belief in my writing still gets me through bad patches.

My thanks goes out to Dan Skoubye of Banda Press International, who was willing to take a risk on a genre of book not often published. I'd like to thank Christy Parr for her work as editor, and Amber Skoubye for her efforts in marketing. I'd also like to thank anyone else on the Banda Press Team who works behind the scenes and may not always be recognized.

I'd like to thank all of the family and friends and co-workers that have shown great enthusiasm about the book, and have worked hard to spread the word about its publication.

And lastly I'd like to thank Tom Lamirand, Jay Jackson, Shawn Morris, and Ryan Rapacz. I've run more miles and shared more memories with these guys than one could hope to dream. Without their support and friendship over the years the ideas that are the soul of this book never would have come to be. Their contribution is limitless.

About the Author

Stephen Paske has always had a love for running. As a young man he ran Cross Country for Osseo Senior High in Minnesota where he was All-State in 1995. From 1996-2000 he competed for Marquette University.

Translating his talent into coaching skills he led Wauwatosa West High School to the Woodland Conference Championship in 2002 and Santa Cruz Cooperative School to the City Track Championship in 2006.

Stephen spends much of his time writing. His articles have appeared in Minnesota Running and Track, Silent Sports, Run Minnesota, Run Michigan, Milwaukee Magazine, and many other publications.

Stephen is now living and teaching in Milwaukee Wisconsin after spending a year in Bolivia.

OTHER

ONE FLIGHT FICTION™

BOOKS AVAILABLE:

Titles	Read Time
Home To Wyoming	0-1 hour read
Perceptions	0-1 hour read
Summersville	1-2 hour read
Dreamers	2-3 hour read
The Looking Glass Call	2-3 hour read

To give us your feedback and learn more about One Flight Fiction™, visit us on the web.

www.OneFlightFiction.com